The Book of the Duchess

Geoffrey Chaucer

Translated by E.B. Richmond

ET REMOTISSIMA PROPE

Hesperus Poetry

Hesperus Poetry
Published by Hesperus Press Limited
4 Rickett Street, London sw6 1RU
www.hesperuspress.com

Middle English text: Benson, Larry D. (General Editor), *The Riverside Chaucer*,
Third Edition. Copyright © 1987 by Houghton Mifflin Company.
Reprinted with permission.
This translation first published by Hesperus Press Limited, 2007

Introduction and English language translation © E.B. Richmond, 2007
Foreword © Bernard O'Donoghue, 2007

Designed and typeset by Fraser Muggeridge studio
Printed in Jordan by Jordan National Press

ISBN: 1-84391-157-4
ISBN13: 978-1-84391-157-9

CONTENTS

FOREWORD

Readers of Chaucer, both in the collected *Works* or in selections, are accustomed to finding the opening of *The Canterbury Tales* on the first page: 'Whan that Aprill with his shoures soote…' It is a wonderful starting point of course; but that fact of itself makes it a hard act to follow. We also need to remind ourselves that it is the opening to Chaucer's latest and most ambitious work, so it is not surprising that most of the poet's other works, following on behind, are seen to pale in comparison. The strange editorial practice has always been to put Chaucer's last and greatest text first, and then go back to the start of his career, continuing from there to present the works chronologically, in so far as that is possible.

If most of Chaucer's writings suffer in the comparison with that brilliant spring opening, the work most disadvantaged by this practice is *The Book of the Duchess*, for two reasons. First, its insomniac opening itself offers a very arresting starting point to a poetic career (Chaucer is very good at openings):

> *I have gret wonder, be this lyght,*
> *How that I lyve, for day ne nyght*
> *I may nat slepe wel nygh noght;*

Secondly, and more obviously, we turn, after all the drama and worldly inventiveness of *The Canterbury Tales*, to the more delicate and remote realm of the medieval love-vision. Its strangeness to us is underlined by the familiarity of all that precedes; then of course we go on to read the rest of Chaucer's works with this dream-world already encountered: this poem takes the strain of the unfamiliar.

For this reason, it is especially welcome to have a new, lively verse translation. E.B. Richmond's version, rendered with the sparkle and fluency of James Joyce's 'Gas from a Burner', enables us to read at the compelling speed that this surreal and swirling dream-narrative demands. Traditional editions of the poem, as in the canon-forming *Riverside Chaucer*, have to place the poem in its context of French dream-vision of the time so we can see exactly what Chaucer is doing with his materials. But this essential activity makes it difficult to *read* the poem in any normal way. It is not just a matter of being unable to read at the appropriate speed, unhampered by footnotes. Even more importantly, to feel what is odd and distinctive and surprising in this dream-narrative, we have to encounter it as a whole, in its own terms, without explaining away particular details.

To take one area where this is particularly crucial: there has always been a critical tendency in readers of medieval love-visions to explain some events in the text by saying 'this is just like a real dream'. As a corrective we need to be reminded that the primary function of the visionary form was to instruct: so in *The Book of the Duchess*, Alcyone prays to Juno for a dream that will tell her reliably about the fate of her husband Ceyx; sure enough, the accurate vision comes to her in sleep. And yet other things in the poem do seem oddly dreamlike. For example when the insomniac narrator finally falls asleep, he dreams he sees a hunt:

I was ryght glad, and up anoon
Took my hors, and forth I wente
Out of my chambre.

Was the horse in the bedroom, as in Laurel and Hardy? Older editions of the poem used to explain this kind of oddness by saying this is early work, written when Chaucer was in his twenties (even the great Chaucer editor F.N. Robinson says that 'the young poet had not yet much thought to contribute or great mastery in expressing it' – a view firmly removed in the *Riverside*). But the more closely you look at the poem, with the closeness that a readily readable translation like this makes easy, the more of this kind of thought-provoking unreality there is. It is clearly a calculated effect.

The poem is full of impossibilities and missed points and people getting the wrong end of the stick. When the narrator learns that Juno through the agency of Morpheus has succeeded in putting Alcyone to sleep, so that she discovers the drowning of her husband and commits suicide, he is completely unmoved by the story's tragedy: he just wants to find Juno so *he* can sleep, without reflecting that this may be to invite tragedy. Similarly, but even more extraordinarily, he seems not to register the fact that the young man in black, whose lament he overhears, is lamenting the loss of his 'lady bright... by death laid low' (though this may be because he assumes that the eleven-line lament he first hears is just a 'lay' or 'song', not referring to the knight's own case – any more than to Chaucer's: the poem used sometimes to be read, rather absurdly, as a piece of poetic autobiography).

There are other odd things too. The poem, for no very obvious reason, is full of numbers – of flowers and stars and trees. Between lines 408 and 425, the specified numbers are 7, 1,000, 10, 12, 40, 50, 1; but the animals are said to be innumerable, even by the decimally informed who can 'rekene and noumbre/and telle of every thing the noumbre'. Neither mathematicians nor the great interpreters of dreams – Macrobius, or Joseph who explained Pharaoh's grim dream – can explain this narrator's dream. So how important is this

ix

dream-encounter? Another puzzle is that the man in black describes his dead lady in the philosophical terms of courtly love, and his life as a kind of battle between Fortune and Nature. If this was Dante speaking of Beatrice, we would be sharply reminded by modern critics that, for all the poem's emotional effectiveness, the lady represents a moral and intellectual force, and that this is not just a lament for a lost duchess. The 'joy' of the encounter with this lady was a matter of learning to transcend an earlier, adolescent love.

The dream of course *does* serve as an elegy for Blanche, Duchess of Lancaster, as the coded lines towards the end show. But for us this is not the primary appeal of this brilliant, bizarre narrative. The lament for the dead lady is only one of the accomplished set pieces of which the poem is composed. The narrating seems more central than the occasion of the poem. The poet admires the knight's complaint (as Chaucer's successor and imitator Lydgate did) as a brilliant poetic exercise rather than an obituary. The man in black stresses to the narrator that 'with heart and mind and soul' he must hear out his tale 'and hear it whole', like the Ancient Mariner seizing on the wedding guest. And this sparkling new translation makes it easy to be captivated by the narrative in this spirit.

– *Bernard O'Donoghue, 2007*

The *Book of the Duchess,* Chaucer's first substantial poem, explores the eternal theme of love and loss through the medium of a dream. Dreams have fascinated the human imagination since the dawn of history, and this fascination is well illustrated by the poetry of western Europe during the high Middle Ages. In France, a favourite type of poetic composition was the *dream-vision*, over which loomed a prodigious allegorical work called the *Roman de la Rose.* This vast production, composed at different times during the thirteenth century by two poets of quite opposing temperaments and viewpoints, was held together by one unifying thread: 'courtly love' (or, as it was known until well into the nineteenth century, *fin' amors*), an extravagantly detailed codification of the rules of behaviour by which aristocratic lovers should at all times be governed. The *Roman* left an indelible mark on medieval poetry as a whole, and Chaucer's not least. Hence it is not surprising that *The Book of the Duchess* should be both a dream-vision and a celebration of *fin' amors* – but here the convention serves the purposes of elegy, while at the same time providing the framework for an incandescent love story. On the surface the poem seems to be telling a story that is simple enough, but its straightforward style masks a considerable complexity, and while few dispute the charm of the poem, many differ as to its interpretation. This introduction gives a brief overview of the story and hopes in so doing to suggest one approach to its understanding.

The factual origin of the poem was almost certainly the death in 1369 of John of Gaunt's first wife, Blanche, Duchess of Lancaster, its purpose being both to commemorate the duchess herself and to console the prince for her loss. Not much is known about the actual relationship between Gaunt, third surviving son of Edward III, and Geoffrey Chaucer, son of a rich wine merchant, whose lifetime of high offices in the king's service meant only that he was always close to the aristocracy but never of it. To be successful in such a life – and Chaucer was extremely successful – required a good deal of discretion, and Chaucer was nothing if not cautious in what he might say about actual personages. For example, in *The Book of the Duchess,* how like Gaunt is its main figure, the man in black? When he first encounters this sorrowful young knight, the dreamer of the poem guesses his age to be about twenty-four years or younger. But scholars today generally agree that Gaunt's age at the time of Blanche's death was twenty-nine. It's been speculated that some scribe's error accounts for the discrepancy – but such an explanation seems unnecessary. What is more likely is that in giving the knight the age he did, Chaucer first of all was simply following the conventions of *fin' amors*, which decreed that romantic lovers must be young, in their middle to late teens or early twenties at most; and secondly, that he had created a red herring that would mitigate any tendency to identify the knight of the poem too closely with the living prince. And so Chaucer cleverly contrived both to distance the man in black from his counterpart in reality, and, by describing that counterpart as a model of rectitude, good looks, and exquisite manners, to pay the prince an indirect but graceful compliment.

The story is as follows: A poet, half dead from sleeplessness and the melancholia caused by an 'eight-years' sickness' (undefined, but by all the logic of the dream-vision a case of unrequited love), tries to forget his misery by losing himself in a book of 'fables'. One of these, an account of the death by shipwreck of King Ceyx, powerfully grips the poet's imagination. This story tells how the despairing queen Alcyone begs Juno, her goddess, either to tell her directly whether the king is alive or dead, or at least to send her sleep, so she might dream, and in that dream see a portent that would reveal the truth. Juno despatches a messenger to the cave of Morpheus, the god of sleep – an episode that hints delightfully at the kind of high comedy that enlivens so many of Chaucer's later poems. Morpheus then leaves his cave, enters the body of the drowned king, and transports it to the bedside of Alcyone. Then and there the apparition tells the queen that she must face the fact that he is finally and forever dead; alas, this truth is more than she can bear, and within three days she, too, is dead. But the king's parting words will resonate throughout the poem: 'To lytel while oure blysse lasteth' ('Too short a time does our joy last').

The insomniac poet at once prays that these hitherto-unheard-of divinities will grant him the same gift they did to the unhappy queen. He, too, is soon plunged into a profound slumber, and his wonderful dream begins. He awakens in a sunlit chamber full of the songs of birds, whose clear glass windows are engraved with the whole story of the *Roman de la Rose*. He hears the sounds of a hunting party and rushes to join it. A hart is found and the hunters give chase, but the hart doubles back, the hounds lose the scent, the party disbands, the dreamer dismounts and a little lost puppy comes snuggling up to him, beguiles him with an irresistible display of canine wooing, and then leads him into a lovely glade where winter's darkness and misery are forgotten in the brightness of recurring spring. The little guide vanishes, and the dreamer wanders on alone into a dense, dark forest full of woodland creatures, until in the forest's darkest depths he comes across a man dressed all in black who, sitting alone with his back against a great oak tree, is singing to himself a pitiful lament for the loss, *through death*, of his beloved lady. Touched, the dreamer courteously makes himself known; the knight responds in kind, and the two begin their long colloquy, in the course of which the hunting of the hart undergoes a metamorphosis: 'hart', figuratively, becomes 'heart', and the chase, no longer a carefree sport with an outward beast in view, continues as a painful search for something entirely inward, even more elusive, and far, far harder to bring to bay.

There is, however, a problem. The words of the dirge-like ballad sung by the man in black and that the dreamer has overheard, have made the cause of his grief unmistakably clear; why, then, during their entire exchange, does the dreamer persist in pretending he does not know the lady is dead?

If the dreamer is not a fool, it must follow that his kindly but relentless questioning of the knight is knowing and purposeful. Their exchange could be read as an early 'talk therapy' session, or, perhaps, as a kind of secular confession, and is remarkable in either case; but could the dreamer also be hoping in this way to learn something that might throw light on his own sufferings? If so, this might explain what appears to be his almost incredible obtuseness – but this is mere speculation. What seems undeniable is that the problem creates a stumbling block in the poem, and as such may be labelled a weakness.

But it is a weakness that seems relatively unimportant when measured against the poem's overweening strengths. Consider, for example, the seamless weaving throughout of the stories of Ceyx and Alcyone and of the hunt; the visual richness of the alternating scenes of light and darkness; the beauty and charm of the descriptions of the magical chamber in which the dreamer awakens, of the forest in which he wanders and of the creatures that inhabit it; and finally, the long, lyrical passage in which the knight's adoration of the lady is often expressed in words that transcend mere praise, and yet, in the spirit of the duchess herself, contain no 'wildness' or folly and whose truth is, therefore, beyond question. In the poem's last lines, moreover, there is a kind of dramatic heightening that foretells the greater mastery to come, for in these lines the dreamer, whatever his motives, does at last succeed in bringing the knight to the point where he is able, without artifice or evasion, to put the cause of his grief into three plain words that until now he could not bring himself to utter: 'She is dead!' With these words the knight, like Alcyone before him, meets the truth head on, with this difference: that the knight's acceptance leads, not to death, but to a life in which raw anguish will give way to a calmer understanding and to memories that death cannot threaten. With these words also, the dreamer's task is finished; why then, should he say any more than he does say: 'By God, it is ruth!' (see note on the translation below).

After this, the horn of the huntsman is heard to signal that there's to be no more 'hunting of the hart' that day. The knight rides home to his castle; his long struggle is over. And what about Gaunt himself? The consolation he is offered appears not to be the consolation of philosophy or religion, but of the knowledge, even stronger than sorrow, that he has experienced one of life's supreme gifts: a fulfilled and perfect love. The poem's portrayal of the duchess might even infuse that knowledge with a measure of joy, for out of it Blanche emerges not only as a paragon of physical and moral beauty, but as a person vividly alive, one whose qualities of honesty, generosity, kindliness, and love of justice and truth are leavened by an extraordinary, even formidable, clear-sightedness as well as by an endearing streak of playfulness and *joie de vivre*. As for the insomniac poet, he awakens from his sleep free from his former misery and eager to begin the pleasurable task of turning his wonderful dream into verse. This he does, and in so doing, quietly propels English poetry some distance along the path to glory.

– *E.B. Richmond, 2007*

Note on the Translation

This rendition attempts to reach a satisfactory compromise between today's language and sensibility and those of Chaucer's own times. I've tried simultaneously to avoid all terms or expressions that would make him seem falsely 'modern', but also all language that would tend to make his poetry seem 'quaint' or archaic to contemporary readers. Even so, in a very few instances, and for lack of adequate equivalents, I've retained Chaucer's exact words without translation. For a long time I hesitated over the dreamer's word 'ruth!' in favour of having him say something like, 'By God, it is a shame!' or 'a pity!' or even some such phrase as, 'By God, I'm sorry!' But in the end, all these alternatives seemed feeble when set against Chaucer's one powerful monosyllable, 'ruth!' We still have the word in the form of the adjective, 'ruthless', which simply means 'without pity'.

By the same token, because in the fourteenth century the use of 'thee/thou' or 'you' as a mode of address was determined by each person's social rank, I've taken a chance on retaining the knight's familiar 'thee/thou' when he speaks to the dreamer and the dreamer's respectful 'you' when he, in turn, addresses the knight. To have both men use 'you' indiscriminately would probably sound more natural to modern ears, yet I'm confident that readers will accept this concession to a custom so integral to the manners of Chaucer's age.

The other places in the poem where I've retained Chaucer's original language (although with modified spelling) are lines 1137–38 and lines 1305–06. These lines do, in fact, simply repeat lines 743–44, which I've rendered as 'My loss goes far beyond, my friend/What thou could'st know or comprehend'; the words of the later lines are: 'Too true; thou know'st not what thou meanest… It is far more than thou weenest', and 'Thou know'st full little what thou meanest; I have lost more than thou weenest'. This thrice-repeated claim forms a kind of leitmotif to the knight's self-revelations, and throws into relief the persistence with which he clings to the notion that the loss he has suffered is utterly beyond any other human being's capacity to understand. It is the last assertion of this obsessive idea that prompts the dreamer's final question, 'Where is she now?' that in turn shocks the knight into his climactic revelation, 'She is dead!' I believe few readers will have any trouble with the word 'weenest', since most are likely to be familiar with the phrase 'I ween' ('I know'), and the words seem to me to carry a weight that translation can do little to improve.

Finally, the greatest liberty I've taken with the poem is to insert a kind of 'gloss' in the form of brief headings that mark off major turning points or changes of subject; these headings are intended to provide breathing room and to make the poem a little easier to follow. If this slight innovation in any way enhances the reader's enjoyment of this early offshoot of a supreme poet's genius, that must do for an excuse.

Acknowledgements

Of the many people who have encouraged me during the preparation of this book, I would like to single out three especially: Steve Ellis, who has been my mentor and guide from the beginning of my work with Chaucer translation and who first urged me to try my hand at *The Book of the Duchess*; John McLaughlin, who has generously read and advised me on my drafts of the poem and the introduction; and my friend Richard Virgil, whose wise counsel has helped keep this effort steadily on course. My greatest debt, however, is to my son, Ben, to whom this book is dedicated with love and thanks.

The Book of the Duchess

I have gret wonder, be this lyght,
How that I lyve, for day ne nyght
I may nat slepe wel nygh noght;
I haveso many an ydel thoght
Purely for defaute of slep
That, by my trouthe, I take no kep
Of nothing, how hyt cometh or gooth,
Ne me nys nothyng leef nor looth.
Al is ylyche good to me –
Joye or sorowe, wherso hyt be –   10
For I have felynge in nothyng,
But as yt were a mased thing,
Always in poynt to falle a-doun;
For sorwful ymagynacioun
Ys alway hooly in my mynde.

 And wel ye woot, agaynes kynde
Hyt were to lyven in thys wyse,
For nature wolde nat suffyse
To noon erthly creature
Nat longe tyme to endure   20
Withoute slep and be in sorwe.
And I ne may, ne nyght ne morwe,
Slepe; and thus melancolye
And drede I have for to dye.
Defaute of slep and hevynesse
Hath sleyn my spirit of quyknesse
That I have lost al lustyhede.
Suche fantasies ben in myn hede
So I not what is best to doo.

 By men might axe me why soo   30

The poet bewails his inability to sleep.

It's a great wonder, by this light
I'm still alive, for day and night
I hardly sleep a single wink,
So many idle thoughts I think.
Purely for lack of sleep, I find,
I can hold nothing in my mind:
Great things may happen, I don't care,
How they began or when or where –
Everything is the same to me,
Joy or sorrow, whatever it be;   10
I've no feeling for anything,
Like a dazed, bewildered thing,
Always about to fall apart,
For sad imagination's art
Wholly preoccupies my mind.
   And well you know, against our kind
And against nature it is to live
Like this, for nature will not give
To any soul on earth, be sure,
Life that will very long endure   20
Both without sleep and full of mourning,
Yet I may not, by night or morning,
Sleep, so in wretchedness must I
Live, and in fear that I must die.
Default of sleep and weight of gloom
Have killed my spirit's life and bloom,
So that I've lost all will to act;
My head is so with fancies wracked
I cannot tell what's best to do.
   But you might ask why this is so   30

I may not slepe and what me is.
But natheles, who aske this
Leseth his asking trewely.
Myselven can not telle why
The sothe; but trewly, as I gesse,
I holde hit be a sicknesse
That I have suffred this eight yeer;
And yet my boote is never the ner,
For there is phisicien but oon+
That may me hele; but that is don. 40
Passe we over untill eft;
That will not be mot need be left;
Our first mater is good to kepe.

So whan I saw I might not slepe
Til now late this other night,
Upon my bed I sat upright
And bad oon reche me a book,
A romaunce, and he it me tok
To rede and drive the night away;
For me thoughte it better play 50
Then playe either at ches or tables.
And in this bok were written fables
The clerkes had in olde tyme,
And other poetes, put in rime
To rede and for to be in minde,
While men loved the lawe of kinde.
This bok ne spak but of such thinges,
Of quenes lives, and of kinges,
And many other thinges smale.
Amonge al this I fond a tale 60
That me thoughte a wonder thing.

That I can't sleep? What's wrong with me?
But all who ask this, he or she,
Will only waste their time, for I
Myself can't tell you how or why,
Or what the truth is; but I guess
It is a sickness, more or less,
That I have suffered these eight years,[1]
Yet still no remedy appears,
For of physicians there's but one
Able to heal me – but that's done.   40
Skip this for now, for past a doubt,
What cannot be must be done without.
To our first subject then let's keep.

    So when I saw I might not sleep
Till very late, the other night,
Upon my bed I sat upright,
And bade my man take down a book,[2]
A romance; this to me he took,
To read and drive the night away –
For sure, I thought it better play   50
Than chess, perhaps, or a game of tables,[3]
And this old book was full of fables
That scholars of an earlier time,
And other poets put in rhyme
For us to read and keep in mind,
When men still loved the law of kind.[4]
This book spoke only of such things
As lives of queens and lives of kings,
And small things I could well pass over,
But then I did at last discover   60
A tale I thought a wondrous thing.

This was the tale: There was a king
That highte Seys, and had a wif,
The beste that mighte bere lyf,
And this quene highte Alcyone.
So it befil thereafter soone
This king wol wenden over see.
To tellen shortly, whan that he
Was in the see thus in this wise,
Such a tempest gan to rise   70
That brak her mast and made it falle,
And clefte her ship, and dreinte hem alle,
That never was founde, as it telles,
Bord ne man, ne nothing elles.
Right thus this king Seys loste his lif.
    Now for to speke of Alycone, his wif:
This lady, that was left at hom,
Hath wonder that the king ne com
Hom, for it was a longe terme.
Anon her herte began to [erme];   80
And for that her thoughte evermo
It was not wele [he dwelte] so,
She longed so after the king
That certes it were a pitous thing
To telle her hertely sorowful lif
That she had, this noble wif,
For him, alas, she loved alderbest.
Anon she sent bothe eest and west
To seke him, but they founde nought.
'Alas!' quod she, 'that I was wrought!'   90

The poet tells the tragic tale of Queen Alcyone and her husband,
King Ceyx.

This was the tale: there was a king
Ceyx by name, who took a wife,
The best that ever was in life,
And this queen's name was Alcyone.
And after this, it chanced quite soon,
The king would venture over sea,
And (to make brief this part) while he
Upon the sea thus bravely goes,
Such a wild hurricane arose   70
It broke their mast, caused it to fall,
Shattered their ship, and drowned them all,
So never was found, the story tells,
Nor plank, nor man, nor nothing else:
Just so, King Ceyx lost his life.
And now of Alcyone his wife
To speak, she that was left at home,
She wondered that he did not come,
Her king, for long had been his leave.
And soon her heart began to grieve,   80
And round and round her thoughts would go
It was not well he lingered so,
So much she longed to see the king,
And sure, it was a piteous thing
To tell of the heart-broken life
This poor queen led, this noble wife,
For above all she loved him best.
At once she sent both east and west
To seek him: they returned with naught.
'Alas!' she cried, 'that I was wrought!   90

And wher my lord, my love, be deed?
Certes, I nil never ete breed,
I make avow to my god here,
But I mowe of my lord here!'
Such sorowe this lady to her tok
That trewly I, that made this book,
Had such pittee and such rowthe
To rede hir sorwe that, by my trowthe,
I ferde the worse al the morwe
Aftir to thenken on hir sorwe.   100

    So whan this lady koude here noo word
That no man myghte fynde hir lord,
Ful ofte she swooned, and sayed 'Alas!'
For sorwe ful nygh wood she was,
Ne she koude no reed but oon;
But doun on knees she sat anoon
And wepte that pittee was to here.

    'A, mercy, swete lady dere!'
Quod she to Juno, hir goddesse,
'Helpe me out of thys distresse,   110
And yeve me grace my lord to se
Soone or wite wher-so he be,
Or how he fareth, or in what wise,
And I shal make yow sacrifise,
And hooly youres become I shal
With good wille, body, herte, and al;
And but thow wolt this, lady swete,
Send me grace to slepe and mete
In my slep som certeyn sweven
Wherthourgh that I may knowen even   120
Whether my lord be quyk or ded.'
    With that word she heng doun the hed

8

And if my lord, my love, be dead,
Truly I'll never more eat bread;
To my high god this do I swear:
Unless of my dear lord I hear!'
Such grief this lady's being shook
That truly I, that made this book,
Felt such pity and such care,
Reading about it, that I swear
All that day I fared the worse
For thinking of her sorrow's curse.   100

So when this queen could get no word
Save that no man could find her lord,
Often she fainted, cried 'Alas!' –
For sorrow well-nigh mad she was.
No plan she knew save only one,
But soon upon her knees fell down,
With weeping pitiful to hear.

'Ah, mercy, my sweet lady dear'
(Juno, her goddess, she thus addressed):
'Help me, who am so sore distressed!   110
Oh, give me grace my lord to see
Soon, or disclose where he may be,
Or how he fares in his emprise,
And I shall be your sacrifice
And wholly yours I'll be, and thrall,
With good will, body, heart, and all;
Or, if too heavy you may deem
This boon, send sleep, that I may dream,
And in that dream a portent see
That shows, past all uncertainty,   120
Whether my lord's alive or dead!'

With that, the queen hung down her head.

And fel a-swowne as cold as ston.
Hyr women kaught hir up anoon
And broghten hir in bed al naked,
And she, forweped and forwaked,
Was wery; and thus the dede slep
Fil on hir or she tooke kep,
Throgh Juno, that had herd hir bone,
That made hir to slepe sone. 130
For as she prayede, ryght so was don
In dede; for Juno ryght anon
Called thus hir messager
To doo hir erande, and he com ner.

Whan he was come, she bad hym thus:
'Go bet,' quod Juno, 'to Morpheus –
Thou knowest hym wel, the god of slep.
Now understond wel and tek kep!
Sey thus on my half: that he
Go faste into the Grete Se, 140
And byd hym that, on alle thyng,
He take up Seys body the kyng,
That lyeth ful pale and nothyng rody.
Bid hym crepe into the body
And doo hit goon to Alcione
The quene, ther she lyeth allone,
 And shewe hir shortly, hit ys no nay,
How hit was dreynt thys other day;
And do the body speke ryght soo,
Ryght as hyt was woned to doo 150
The whiles that hit was alyve.

Soon her exhausted, wasted frame
Fell in a faint; her women came,
And brought her naked to her bed,
But she'd no tears; they'd all been shed.
So wan she was, so full of care,
A dead sleep took her unaware
From Juno, who had heard her moan,
And gave her sleep, that blessed boon,   130
For, as she prayed, so it was done
In very deed; Juno upon
That word called forth her messenger
To do her will; he came to her.

On Juno's command, the messenger visits the cave of Morpheus.

When he had come, she bade him thus:
'Go fast,' she said, 'to Morpheus,
The god of sleep well known indeed
To you: now hear me and take heed!
Say this on my behalf, that he
Shall go at once to the Great Sea,[5]   140
And, above all, this order bring,
That he must take up Ceyx the king
Who lies so pale, in nothing ruddy;
Then bid him creep into the body,
And make it go to Alcyone
The queen, where now she lies alone,
And show her then and there, I say,
How it was drowned the other day,
And make it speak in words just so
As ever was its wont to do   150
Before, while it was still alive.

Goo now faste, and hye the blyve!'

This messager tok leve and wente
Upon hys wey, and never ne stente
Til he com to the derke valeye
That stant betwixte roches tweye
Ther never yet grew corn ne gras,
Ne tre, ne noght that ought was,
Beste, ne man, ne noght elles,
Save ther were a fewe welles   160
Came rennynge fro the clyves adoun,
That made a dedly slepynge soun,
And ronnen doun ryght by a cave
That was under a rokke ygrave
Amydde the valey, wonder depe.
There these goddes lay and slepe,
Morpheus and Eclympasteyr,
That was the god of slepes heyr,
That slep and dide no other werk.
This cave was also as derk   170
As helle-pit overall aboute.
They had good leyser for to route,
To envye who myghte slepe best.
Somme henge her chyn upon hir brest
And slept upryght, hir hed yhed,
And somme lay naked in her bed
And slepe whiles the dayes laste.

The messager com fleynge faste
And cried, 'O, how! Awake anoon!'
Hit was for noght; there herde him non.   180
'Awake!' quod he, 'whoo ys lyth there?'
And blew his horn right in here eere,
And cried 'Awaketh!' wonder hyë.

Go now, and may your mission thrive!'
   No whit this messenger delayed,
Took leave, and neither stopped nor stayed
Till a dark valley came in view
Between two vast cliffs grey of hue;
No grass or trees or corn grew there,
Of living things these rocks were bare,
Of man or beast, and all things else,
Save that, high up, were certain wells   160
That from the cliffs flowed toward the ground,
Making a deathlike, slumbrous sound.
Right by a cave these waters passed,
Carved underneath those boulders vast
Within the valley, wondrous deep,
Wherein the gods lay fast asleep –
Morpheus and Eclympasteyr,
The god of sleep's own son and heir,
Who slept and did no other work.
Also this cave was dim with murk   170
As is hell's pit for ever more;
The gods had ample time to snore,
To try which one might sleep the best.
Some hung their chin upon their breast,
And slept upright with covered heads,
And some lay naked on their beds,
Sleeping as long as day might last.
   The messenger came flying fast,
And cried, 'Ho, there! wake up, good sirs!'
But all in vain, for no one stirs.   180
'Wake up!' he cried, 'Who slumbers here?'
And blew his horn right in his ear.
'Wake up!' he cried, both loud and high.

This god of slep with hys oon yë
Cast up, and axed, 'Who clepeth ther?'
   'Hyt am I,' quod this messager.
'Juno bad thow shuldest goon' –
And tolde hym what he shulde doon
(As I have told yow here-to-fore;
Hyt ys no need reherse hyt more)   190
And went hys wey whan he had sayd.
Anoon this god of slep abrayd
Out of hys slep, and gan to goon,
And dyde as he had bede hym doon:
Took up the dreynte body sone
And bar hyte forth to Alcione,
Hys wife the quene, ther as she lay
Ryght even a quarter before day,
And stood ryght at hyr beddes fet,
And called her ryght as she het   200
By name, and sayde, 'My swete wyf,
Awake! Let be your sorwful lyf,
For in your sorwe there lyth no red;
For, certes, swete, I am but ded.
Ye shul me never on lyve yse.
But, goode swete herte, that ye
Bury my body, for such a tyde
Ye mowe hyt fynde the see besyde;
And farewel, swete, my worldes blysse!
I praye God youre sorwe lysse.   210
To lytel while oure blysse lasteth!'
   With that her eyen up she casteth
And saw noght. 'Allas!' quod she for sorwe,
And deyede within the thridde morwe.
But what she sayede more in that swow

14

The god of sleep then, with one eye
Looked up and asked, 'Who's calling there?'
    'It's I,' then said the messenger,
'Juno commands that you should go' –
And told him then what he must do
As I have told to you before,
So I need not rehearse it more,   190
And, having spoken, he departed.
Quickly the god of slumber started
Out of his sleep, began to go,
And did as he'd been bid to do;
Took the drowned body up and soon
Carried it straight to Alcyone
His wife, the good queen, where she lay,
Three hours before the break of day;
Stood at the foot of her bed frame,
Spoke to her by her own right name,   200
And said to her, 'My sweet, dear wife,
Awake! give up your tearful life:
For this your sorrow there's no cure,
For truly, sweet, I'm dead for sure.
Never alive you'll see me more,
But, good, sweet heart, I now implore,
Bury my body, which you'll see
Quite soon, stretched out beside the sea.
Farewell, my world's sole bliss! I pray
God may in time your grief allay.   210
Too short a time does our joy last!'
    With that, the queen her eyes upcast,
And nothing saw. 'Alas!' for sorrow
She cried, and died on the third morrow.
What more she said in that despair

I may not telle yow as now;
Hyt were to longe for to dwelle.

My first matere I wil yow telle,
Wherfore I have told this thyng
Of Alcione and Seys the kyng,   220
For thus moche dar I saye wel:
I had be dolven everydel
And ded, ryght thurgh defaute of slep,
Yif I ne had red and take kep
Of this tale next before.
And I wol telle yow wherfore:
For I ne myghte, for bote ne bale,
Slepe or I had red thys tale
Of this dreynte Seys the kyng
And of the goddes of slepyng.   230
    When I had red thys tale wel
And overloked hyt everydel,
Me thoghte wonder yf hit were so,
For I had never herd speke or tho
Of noo goddes that koude make
Men to slepe, ne for to wake,
For I ne knew never god but oon,
And in my game I sayde anoon
(And yet my lyst ryght evel to playe)
Rather then that y shulde deye   240
Thorgh defaute of slepynge thus,
I wolde yive thilke Morpheus,
Or hys goddesse, dame Juno,

I may not tell you now; it were
Too long – I may not on it dwell.

The poet, still wakeful, entertains fancies about
what he'd do if sleep were only granted him.

Of my first subject I shall tell
And why I've told you this sad thing
Of Alcyone and Ceyx the king,   220
For this much I dare say as well:
I'd have been buried, gone to hell,
And died for lack of sleep, indeed,
Had I not read and taken heed
Of this old tale I told just now,
And I will tell you why and how,
For I might not, for God's own glory,
Sleep, if I'd not read this story
Of Ceyx, who pitifully was drowned,
And of the gods of sleep profound.   230
    When thoroughly I'd read this tale,
And weighed and pondered each detail,
I thought it strange if it were true,
For I had never, hitherto,
Heard of a god who so could make
People to sleep or stay awake,
For only one god had I known.
I said then (playing the buffoon,
Though I'd no wish at all to play),
Rather than I should die straightway,   240
If things with me continued thus,
I'd give to this god Morpheus
And to his goddess Juno, too,

Or som wight elles, I ne roghte who –
'To make me slepe and have som reste
I wil yive hym the alderbeste
Yifte that ever he abod hys lyve.
And here on warde, ryght now as blyve,
Yif he wol make me slepe a lyte,
Of down of pure dowves white   250
I will yive hym a fether-bed,
Rayed with gold and ryght wel cled
In fyn blak satyn doutremer,
And many a pilowe, and every ber
Of cloth of Reynes, to slepe softe –
Hym that nor need to turnen ofte –
And I wol yive hym al that falles
To a chambre, and al hys halles
I wol do peynte with pure gold
And tapite hem ful many fold   260
Of oo sute; this shal he have
(Yf I wiste where were hys cave),
Yf he kan make me slepe sone,
As did the goddesse quene Alcione.
And thus this ylke god, Morpheus,
May wynne of me moo feës thus
Than ever he wan; and to Juno,
That ys hys goddesse, I shal soo do,
I trow, that she shal holde hir payd.'

    I hadde unneth that word ysayd   270
Ryght thus as I have told hyt yow,
That sodeynly, I nyste how,
Such a lust anoon me took
To slepe that ryght upon my book
Y fil aslepe, and therwith even

18

Or anyone, I know not who,
'To make me sleep and have some rest,
I'll give to him the very best
Gift he could ever hope to get,
At once, this minute, sooner yet,
If he will make me sleep one night.
Of down of doves, so soft and white   250
I'll give him a fine feather bed
Striped with gold leaf, and right well clad
In fine black satin from far-off places,
And many pillows and pillowcases
Of cloth so soothing to his head
He'll never toss and turn in bed;
And all things that are fitting for
A bedchamber I'll give and more;
His halls I'll paint with purest gold,
Hang tapestries with many a fold   260
Of matching kinds: this shall he have
(If I only I could find his cave),
If he could make me sleep and soon,
As did the goddess Queen Alcyone.
If so, this god, this Morpheus,
May win of me more tribute thus
Than ever he won; for Juno, too,
His goddess, like things will I do –
I swear, she'll think herself well paid.'

Well, those last words were hardly said   270
That I've set down for you just now,
When suddenly, I don't know how,
Such lust for slumber overtook
My soul, that right upon my book,
My head fell down, and then and there

19

Me mette so ynly swete a sweven,
So wonderful that never yit
Y trowe no man had the wyt
To konne wel my sweven rede;
No, not Joseph, withoute drede,   280
Of Egipte, he that redde so
The kynges metynge Pharao,
No more than koude the lest of us;
Ne nat skarsly Macrobeus
(He that wrot al th'avysyoun
That he mette, kyng Scipioun,
The noble man, the Affrikan –
Such marvayles fortuned than),
I trowe, arede my dremes even.
Loo, thus hyt was; thys was my sweven.   290

   Me thoghte thus; that hyt was May,
And in the dawenynge I lay
(Me mette thus) in my bed al naked
And loked forth, for I was waked
With smale foules a gret hep
That had affrayed me out of my slep
Thorgh noyse and swetnesse of her song.
And, as me mette, they sate among
Upon my chambre roof wythoute,
Upon the tyles, overall aboute,   300
And songe, everych in hys wyse,
The moste solempne servise
By noote that ever man, y trowe,

I dreamed a dream so sweet and fair,
So wonderful, that never yet
Has mortal being had the wit
Its meaning quite to ravel out;
No, not Joseph, without doubt, 280
He that in Egypt portents read
And Pharoah's dreams interpreted,
No more than could the least of us;
Not even wise Macrobius[6]
Who wrote so fully long ago
About the dream of Scipio –
That noble man, the 'African'[7] –
Because such marvels happened then,
Could grasp its meaning whole, I deem;
Here's how it was, then: here's my dream. 290

The dreamer imagines himself in a painted chamber
filled with the songs of innumerable birds.

I thought it was the month of May,
And in the dawning light I lay
(I dreamt thus) naked in my bed,
And then looked up, for sleep had fled,
At sound of small birds a great heap,
Who'd startled me out of my sleep
Through noise and sweetness of their song,
And in my dream, there came a throng
Upon the roof and in the air,
Upon the tiles and everywhere, 300
And sang, each one in his own key,
A Mass of more solemnity
And harmony, than men, I vow,

Had herd, for som of hem song lowe,
Som high, and al of oon acord.
To telle shortly, att oo word,
Was never herd so swete a steven
But hyt had be a thyng of heven –
So mery a soun, so swete entewnes,
That certes, for the toun of Tewnes   310
I nolde but I had herd hem synge;
For al my chambre gan to rynge
Thurgh syngynge of her armonye;
For instrument nor melodye
Was nowhere herd yet half so swete,
Nor of acord half so mete;
For ther was noon of hem that feyned
To synge, for ech of hem hym peyned
To fynde out mery crafty notes.
They ne spared not her throtes.   320
And sooth to seyn, my chambre was
Ful wel depeynted, and with glas
Were al the wyndowes wel yglased
Ful clere, and nat an hole ycrased,
That to beholde hyt was gret joye.
For hooly al the story of Troye
Was in the glasynge ywroght thus,
Of Ector and of kyng Priamus,
Of Achilles and of kyng Lamedon,
And eke of Medea and of Jason,   330
Of Paris, Eleyne, and of Lavyne.
And alle the walles with colours fyne
Were peynted, bothe text and glose,
Of al the Romaunce of the Rose.
My wyndowes were shette echon,

Had heard on earth, for some sang low,
Some high, and all of one accord,
And, to speak briefly in a word,
Never was heard such glorious voices
Save those in which high heaven rejoices.
So glad the sound, so sweet the tune is,
I'd give up all the wealth of Tunis   310
Just for a chance to hear them sing.
All my chamber began to ring
By reason of their harmony;
For, instrument nor melody,
Never was heard so sweet, so pure,
Nor, in their notes' accord, so sure;
For there was none among them feigning
His song, for each of them was straining
To find still more ingenious notes,
And so they did not spare their throats.   320
Now, truth to tell, my chamber was
Most finely painted, and with glass
My windows shone most bright and clear,
Nor did a single crack appear,
And to behold it was great joy,
For the whole history of Troy
Was fully etched upon the glass;
Of Hector and King Priamus.
Of Achilles and King Lamedon,[8]
And of Medea and Aeson's son,[9]   330
Paris, Helena, Lavinia[10] too,
And all the walls in colours true,
Depicted both the text and glose[11]
Of the whole *Roman de la Rose*.
My windows now were shut, each one,

And throgh the glas the sonne shon
Upon my bed with bryghte bemes,
With many glade gilde stremes;
And eke the welken was so fair –
Blew, bright, clere was the ayr,   340
And ful attempre for soothe hyt was;
For nother to cold nor hoot yt nas,
Ne in al the welken was a clowde.

As I lay thus, wonder lowde
Me thoght I herde an hunte blowe
T'assay hys horn and for to knowe
Whether hyt were clere or hors of soun.
And I herde goynge bothe up and doun
Men, hors, houndes, and other thyng;
And al men speken of hunting,   350
How they wolde slee the hert with strengthe,
And how the hert had upon lengthe
So moche embrosed – y not now what.
    Anoon ryght whan I herde that,
How that they wolde on-huntynge goon,
I was ryght glad, and up anoon
Took my hors, and forth I wente
Out of my chambre; I never stente
Til I com to the feld withoute.
Ther overtook y a gret route   360
Of huntes and eke of foresteres,
With many relayes and lymeres,
And hyed hem to the forest faste

And through the glass the bright sun shone
Upon my bed with radiant beams
In many glad and golden streams,
And, too, the heavens showed so fair:
Blue, bright, and clear was all the air,   340
And temperate too, if truth be told,
Neither too hot nor yet too cold,
Nor in the sky a single cloud.

The dreamer joins a hunting party; the quarry escapes; a lost
puppy appears and leads the dreamer into another wood.

   And as I lay there, wondrous loud
I thought I heard a huntsman blow
His horn, to test it and to know
Whether its sound was clear or no;
And I heard, going to and fro,
Men, horses, hounds, with all their gear,
And all men spoke of hunting there: 350
How they would slay the hart with strength,
And how the creature would at length
Be wearied out – I don't know what.
   Well, then, at once, when I heard that,
How to the chase they soon would trot,
It made me glad, and up I got,
Took horse and rode away with speed,
And never once restrained my steed
Until I reached the field without,
And overtook there a great rout   360
Of hunters, foresters, hounds unspent,
And hounds long used to hunt by scent,
And to the forest all rode fast,

And I with hem. So at the laste
I asked oon, ladde a lymere:
'Say, felowe, who shal hunte here?'
Quod I, and he answered ageyn,
    'Syr, th'emperour Octovyen,'
Quod he, 'and ys here faste by.'
    'A Goddes half, in good tyme!' quod I,   370
'Go we faste!' and gan to ryde.
Whan we came to the forest syde,
Every man dide ryght anoon
As to huntynge fil to doon.
The master-hunte anoon, fot-hot,
With a gret horn blew thre mot
At the uncouplynge of hys houndes.
Withynne a while the hert yfounde ys,
Yhalowed, and rechased faste
Longe tyme; and so at the laste   380
This hert rused and staal away
Fro alle the houndes a privy way.
The houndes had overshote hym alle
And were on a defaute yfalle.
Therwyth the hunte wonder faste
Blew a forloyn at the laste.
    I was go walked fro my tree,
And as I wente, ther cam by mee
A whelp, that fauned me as I stood,
That hadde yfolowed and koude no good.   390
Hyt com and crepte to me as lowe
Ryght as hyt hadde me yknowe,
Helde doun hys hed and joyned hys eres,
And leyde al smothe doun hys heres.
I wolde have kaught hyt, and anoon

And I with them, and so at last,
To one who led a dog pure-bred,
'Say, fellow, who hunts here?' I said.
The boy then answered me again,
 'Sir, it's the Emperor Octavian,[12]
And he is here and quite nearby.'
 'By God, a timely thought,' said I,   370
'Let's get a move on, boy, and ride!'
When we came to the forest side,
Each man checked his gear and stood
Ready, as every hunter should.
The master huntsman quickly blew
Three blasts that wound the woodland through
As he uncoupled each strong hound,
And soon enough a hart they found.
The hunters cried, 'Halloo!' and fast
And long they chased it, but at last   380
It doubled back and stole away
From the pursuit a secret way.
The hounds had overshot their prey
And lost the scent and ceased to bay.
The master blew the notes that told
His men the trail had now grown cold.

 I walked away then from my tree,
And as I walked, there came to me
A whelp who fawned on me, and who
Followed, and knew not what to do.   390
He crept to me as meek and low
As if he'd known me long ago,
Held down his head, laid back his ears,
And smooth and flat made all his hairs.
I would have caught him up, but soon

Hyt fledde and was fro me goon;
And I hym folwed, and hyt forth wente
Doun by a floury grene wente
Ful thikke of gras, ful softe and swete.
With floures fele, faire under fete,   400
And litel used; hyt semed thus,
For both Flora and Zephirus,
They two that make floures growe,
Had mad her dwellynge ther, I trowe;
For hit was, on to beholde,
As thogh the erthe envye wolde
To be gayer than the heven,
To have moo floures, swiche seven,
As in the welken sterres bee.
Hyt had forgete the povertee   410
That winter, thorgh hys colde morwes,
Had mad hyt suffre, and his sorwes;
All was forgeten, and that was sene,
For al the woode was waxen grene;
Swetnesse of dew had mad hyt waxe.

   Hyt ys no nede eke for to axe
Wher there were many grene greves,
Or thikke of trees, so ful of leves;
And every tree stood by hymselve
Fro other wel ten foot or twelve –   420
So grete trees, so huge of strengthe,
Of fourty or fifty fadme lengthe,
Clene withoute bowgh or stikke,
With croppes brode, and eke as thikke –
They were nat an ynche asonder –
That hit was shadewe overal under.
And many an hert and many an hynde

He ran off and was quickly gone,
I after him, and he next was seen
Down in a blossoming alley green,
With grasses thick and soft and sweet,
With flowers fair beneath my feet,   400
And little used, I'm sure, by us
Of human kind, for Zephyrus[13]
And Flora, who make the flowers grow,
Made it their dwelling here below,
For, to behold it was as though
The earth wished ardently to show
She could be gayer than the heaven,
And have more flowers – yes, more than seven
Times as many as stars in sky.
She had forgot the poverty   410
That winter, with its ice and snow
Had made her suffer, and all its woe;
All was forgotten, as was well seen,
For all the woods again were green:
Sweetness of dew had done its task.

 No need for anyone to ask
Whether a thousand branches grew
Thick on the trees, all green of hue,
For every tree stood by itself
Set off from others ten feet or twelve;   420
Such mighty trees, so huge in strength,
Of forty or fifty fathoms' length,
Yet without branch or twig or stick
But crowned with a canopy too thick
To let in one small gleam or spark
Of light, so all beneath was dark.
And many a hart and many a hind

Was both before me and behynde.
Of founes, sowres, bukkes, does
Was ful the woode, and many roes,   430
And many sqwirelles that sete
Ful high upon the trees and ete,
And in hir maner made festes.
Shortly, hyt was so ful of bestes
That thogh Argus, the noble countour,
Sete to rekene in hys countour,
And rekene with his figures ten –
For by tho figures mowe al ken,
Yf they be crafty, rekene and noumbre,
And telle of every thing the noumbre –   440
Yet shoulde he fayle to rekene even
The wondres me mette in my swevene.

    But forth they romed ryght wonder faste
Doun the woode; so at the laste
I was war of a man in blak,
Than sat and had yturned his bak
To an ook, an huge tree.
'Lord,' thoght I, 'who may that be?
What ayleth hym to sitten her?'
Anoon-ryght I wente ner;   450
Than found I sitte even upryght
A wonder wel-farynge knyght –
By the maner me thoghte so –
Of good mochel, and ryght yong therto,
Of the age of foure and twenty yer,
Upon hys berd but lytel her,

Went both before me and behind –
Of fawns, bucks young and old, and does
The wood was full, and many roes,   430
And many squirrels who nibbled fast
High up, their nuts and forest mast,
And in their way, observed their feasts.
And soon, it was so full of beasts
That even if Algus,[14] paramount
In numbers, should sit down and count,
Reckoning by his number, 'ten' –
For by such figures now all men
With wit enough, can calculate,
Add, multiply, enumerate –   440
Yet would he fail to reckon right
The wonders that I dreamed that night.

The dreamer encounters a man dressed all in black.

But on they roamed, so wondrous fast,
Deep in the woods, and then at last
I grew aware of a man in black,
Sitting alone, that had his back
Pressed against a huge old tree;
And, 'Lord,' I thought, 'who may that be?
What ails him to be sitting there?'
And so, straight off, I ventured near,   450
And found, thus sitting there erect,
A knight well-looking and correct –
By his carriage I thought him so –
And well-proportioned, and young also;
Twenty-four years I guessed he had,
Almost, indeed, a beardless lad,

And he was clothed al in blak.
I stalked even unto hys bak,
And there I stood as stille as ought,
That, soth to saye, he saw me nought;   460
For-why he heng hys hed adoun,
And with a dedly sorwful soun
He made of rym ten vers or twelve
Of a compleynte to hymselve –
The moste pitee, the moste rowthe,
That ever I herde; for, by my trowthe,
Hit was gret wonder that Nature
Myght suffre any creature
To have such sorwe and be not ded.
Ful pitous pale and nothyng red,   470
He sayd a lay, a maner song,
Withoute noote, withoute song;
And was thys, for ful wel I kan
Reherse hyt; ryght thus hyt began:

   'I have sorwe so gret won
That joye gete I never non,
Now that I see my lady bryght,
Which I have loved with al my myght,
Is fro me ded and ys agoon.
   'Allas, deth, what ayleth the,   480
That thou noldest have taken me,
Whan thou toke my lady swete,
That was so fair, so fresh, so fre,
So good that men may wel se
Of al goodnesse she had no mete!'

And dressed from head to toe in black.
I tiptoed then behind his back,
And, silent as a stone, stood there.
He did not see me, I could swear, 460
Because his head was drooping so,
And with a sound dirge-like and low,
Some dozen lines began to make
Of a complaint[15] for his own sake.
It was more pitiful, I guess,
Than ever I heard; and I confess
I was amazed that Nature could
Let any creature, bad or good,
Suffer such pain, and not be dead.
Pale, in his cheeks no trace of red, 470
He sang a lay, a kind of song
Without notes, and without song;[16]
And it was this, for well I can
Remember it: thus it began:

'I have such sorrow and such woe
That joy I never more shall know,
Now that I see my lady bright
Whom I have loved with all my might,
Is gone from me, by death laid low.
'O death, alas, what aileth thee, 480
Why could'st thou not have taken me
When thou didst take my lady sweet,
That was so fair, so fresh, so free,
So good that all the world might see
Such goodness none could match nor meet?'

Whan he had mad thus his complaynte,
Hys sorwful hert gan faste faynte
And his spirites wexen dede;
The blood was fled for pure drede   490
Doun to hys herte, to make him warm –
For wel hyt feled the herte had harm –
To wite eke why hyt was adrad
By kynde, and for to make hyt glad,
For hit ys membre principal
Of the body; and that made al
Hys hewe change and wexe grene
And pale, for ther noo blood ys sene
In no maner lym of hys.
Anoon therwith whan y sawgh this –   500
He ferde thus evel there he set –
I went and stood ryght at his fet,
And grette hym; but he spak noght,
But argued with his owne thoght,
And in hys wyt disputed faste
Why and how hys lyf myght laste;
Hym thoughte hys sorwes were so smerte
And lay so colde upon hys herte.
So, throgh hys sorwe and hevy thoght,
Made hym that he herde me noght;   510
For he had wel nygh lost hys mynde,
Thogh Pan, that men clepeth god of kynde,
Were for hys sorwes never so wroth.

But at the last, to sayn ryght soth,
He was war of me, how y stood
Before hym and did of myn hood,
And had ygret hym as I best koude,
Debonayrly, and nothyng lowde.

When he had done with his complaint,
His sorrowful heart began to faint.
Death then upon his spirit lay,
And terror drove his blood straightway   490
Down to his heart, to make him warm,
(For well it knew the heart had harm)
To search the nature of his fear,
In hope to bring him better cheer,
Seeing it is of organs all
Within the body the principal,
Changing men's hue from red to green
Or pale, when no blood may be seen
In any part or limb of his.
And now, when I perceived all this –   500
How ill he grew in his oaken seat –
I went and stood before his feet
To greet him, but no word he said,
But still debated in his head,
And round and round his mind he cast
To know, to what end his life should last,
Because he thought his grief too sore
That lay so cold at his heart's core;
And, sunk so deep in thought and pain,
He could not hear me; I spoke in vain,   510
For he had nearly lost his mind,
Nor cared if Pan, the god of kind,[17]
Were never so angry at his dismay.

But then, at last, the truth to say,
He grew aware of how I stood
Before him. I took off my hood,
And greeted him as best I could,
With courtesy and voice subdued.

He sayde, 'I pray the, be not wroth.
I herde the not, to seyn the soth,   520
Ne I sawgh the not, syr, trewely.'

  'A, goode sir, no fors,' quod y,
'I am ryght sory yif I have ought
Destroubled yow out of your thought.
Foryive me, yif I have mystake.'

  'Yis, th'amendes is lyght to make,'
Quod he, 'for ther lyeth noon therto;
There ys nothyng myssayd nor do.'

  Loo, how goodly spak thys knyght,
As hit had be another wyght;   530
He made hyt nouther towgh ne queynte.
And I saw that, and gan me aqueynte
With hym, and fond hym so tretable,
Ryght wonder skylful and resonable,
As me thoghte, for al hys bale,
Anoon ryght I gan fynde a tale
To hym, to loke wher I myght ought
Have more knowynge of hys thought.
'Sir,' quod I, 'this game is doon.
'I holde that this hert be goon;   540
These huntes konne hym nowher see.'

  'Y do no fors therof,' quod he;
My thought ys theron never a del,'

  'By oure Lord,' quod I, 'y trow yow wel;
Ryght so me thinketh by youre chere.
But, sir, oo thyng wol ye here?
Me thynketh in gret sorowe I yow see;
But certes, sire, yif that yee
Wolde ought discure me youre woo,
I wolde, as wys God helpe me soo,   550

He said, 'Pray, don't be angry, sir;
To tell the truth, I did not hear 520
Or even see thee, standing by.'

   'It does not matter, sir,' said I,
'And I am sorry if in aught
I have disturbed you in your thought;
Forgive me if I've made mistake.'

   'Yes – the amends are light to make,'
Said he, 'for truly, there are none,
And nothing wrong's been said or done.'

   How kindly spoke this knight, look you,
As any lesser man might do; 530
In no way proud, aloof, or vain,
And seeing this, I sought to gain
His trust, and found him affable,
In speech so sane and reasonable
Despite the pain that he endured,
That I began, thus reassured,
To cast about how I might find
A better knowledge of his mind.
'Sir,' then I said, 'the sport is done,
And I believe the hart is gone – 540
The hunt has seen no sign of it.'

   Said he, 'I do not care a bit.
Never on that could my thoughts dwell.'

   'By God,' said I, 'I saw that well,
And in your face so drawn and drear;
But, sir, would you this one thing hear?
I think your anguish I can see,
But I can tell you certainly,
If in my ear you would disclose
The nature of it, then, God knows, 550

37

Amende hyt, yif I kan or may.
Ye mowe preve hyt be assay;
For, by my trouthe, to make yow hool
I wol do al my power hool.
And telleth me of your sorwes smerte;
Paraunter hyt may ese youre herte,
That semeth ful sek under your syde.'

With that he loked on me asyde,
As who sayth, 'Nay, that wol not be.'
'Graunt mercy, goode frend,' quod he,   560
'I thanke the that thow woldest soo,
But hyt may never the rather be doo.
No man may my sorwe glade,
That maketh my hewe to falle and fade,
And hath myn understondynge lorn
That me ys wo that I was born!
May noght make my sorwes slyde,
Nought al the remedyes of Ovyde,
Ne Orpheus, god of melodye,
Ne Dedalus with his playes slye;   570
Ne hele me may no phisicien,
Noght Ypocras ne Galyen;
Me ys wo that I lyve houres twelve.
But whooso wol assay hymselve
Whether his hert kan have pitee
Of any sorwe, lat hym see me.
Y wrecche, that deth hath mad al naked
Of al the blysse that ever was maked,
Yworthe worste of alle wyghtes,

To ease it, sir, I'd do my best –
This you may put to any test –
For, by my faith, to see you mend,
All of my skill I would expend.
Then tell me of your sorrow's smart –
Perhaps, sir, it would ease your heart,
Whose beat now sounds so weak and scant.'

Pouring forth his grief, the knight rails against Fortune.

With that, he looked at me aslant,
As one who says, 'that cannot be.'
'I'm grateful to thee, friend,' said he,   560
'Thanks for the good will thou hast shown;
And yet it won't be sooner done.
No man can lift my sorrow's pall
That makes my colour fade and fall,
And leaves my mind so lost and lorn
I rue the day that I was born!
Nothing shall give my sorrow ease –
Not all of Ovid's remedies,[18]
Nor Orpheus' lyre, Music's child,[19]
Nor Daedalus' skills heaped up and piled;[20]   570
Nor may physicians give surcease –
Not Galen nor Hippocrates.[21]
I'm loath to live twelve hours more,
But he who would his heart explore
To learn if in some small degree
It felt for grief, let him see me,
I wretched, that death has stripped so bare
Of all the joys that ever were,
Become the worst in all men's eyes,

That hate my dayes and my nyghtes! 580
My lyf, my lustes, be me loothe,
For al welfare and I be wroothe.
The pure deth ys so ful my foo
That I wolde deye, hyt wolde not soo;
For whan I folwe hyt, hit wol flee;
I wolde have hym, hyt nyl nat me.
This ys my peyne wythoute red,
Alway deynge and be not ded,
That Cesiphus, that lyeth in helle,
May not of more sorwe telle. 590
And whoso wiste al, by my trouthe,
My sorwe, but he hadde rowthe
And pitee of my sorwes smerte,
That man hath a fendly herte;
For whoso seeth me first on morwe
May seyn he hath met with sorwe,
For y am sorwe, and sorwe ys y.

'Allas! and I wol tel the why:
My song ys turned to pleynynge,
And al my laughtre to wepynge, 600
My glade thoghtes to hevynesse;
In travayle ys myn ydelnesse
And eke my reste; my wele is woo,
My good ys harm, and evermoo
In wrathe ys turned my pleynge
And my delyt into sorwynge.
Myn hele ys turned into seknesse,
In drede ys al my sykernesse;
To derke ys turned al my lyght,
My wyt ys foly, my day ys nyght, 610
My love ys hate, my slep wakynge,

40

I, who my days and nights despise!   580
What's left of life is bitter lees,
All health and I are enemies,
And death's become so much my foe
That, would I die, it would not so,
For when I follow it, it will flee –
I'd fain have him, he'll not have me.
This is my pain, as I have said,
Always dying and never dead,
So much that Sisyphus in hell[22]
May not of greater torment tell,   590
And he who all my sorrow knew,
And did not grieve, and felt no rue
For pity of my sorrow's smart,
That man must have a fiend-like heart,
For he who first, upon the morrow,
Meets me, may say that he's met sorrow,
For I am sorrow, and sorrow I.
    'Alas, and I will tell thee why
My song has turned into lament,
And into tears my merriment,   600
My happy thoughts to heaviness,
My idle hours to toil and stress,
Likewise my sleep; my bliss is blight,
My good is bad, and day and night
My play has turned into chagrin,
To pain all I delighted in;
My health to sickness unto death,
To fear my certainty and faith;
To darkness has turned all my light,
My wit is folly, my day is night,   610
My love is hate; awake I sleep,

My myrthe and meles ys fastynge,
My countenaunce ys nycete
And al abaved, where so I be;
My pees in pledynge and in werre.
Allas, how myghte I fare werre?
My boldnesse ys turned to shame,
For fals Fortune hath pleyd a game
Atte ches with me, allas the while!
The trayteresse fals and ful of gyle,   620
That al behoteth and nothyng halt,
She goth upryght and yet she halt,
That baggeth foule and loketh faire,
The dispitouse debonaire
That skorneth many a creature!
An ydole of fals portrayture
Ys she, for she wol sone wrien;
She is the monstres hed ywrien,
As fylthe over-ystrawed with floures.
Hir moste worshippe and hir flour ys   630
To lyen, for that ys hyr nature;
Withoute feyth, lawe, or mesure
She ys fals, and ever laughynge
With oon eye, and that other wepynge.
That ys broght up she set al doun.
I lykne hyr to the scorpioun,
That ys a fals, flaterynge beste,
For with his hed he maketh feste,
But al amydde hys flaterynge
With hys tayle he wol stynge   640
And envenyme; and so wol she.
She ys th'envyouse charite
That ys ay fals and semeth wel;

42

Dining I fast, in mirth I weep,
My looks abashed which once were free,
Distraught wherever I may be,
In war and wrangling my peace now is –
Oh, could a man fare worse than this?
My boldness now has turned to shame,
For Fortune the False has played a game
Of chess with me, alas the while!
That traitoress false and full of guile,   620
That promises all, yet nothing pays,
Walks upright, yet with dragging pace,
That squints so foul and looks so fair
That proud, disdainful *debonaire,*
Whose scorn so many souls endure!
An idol of false portraiture
Is she, who so quickly turns aside,
Who well her monster's head can hide,
Like filth with flowers overlaid.
Her highest honour, her accolade,   630
It is to lie; her natural pleasure,
Having no faith, no law, no measure.
She'll laugh, that false one, with one eye,
And with the other she will cry.
Whatever's up, she'll bring it down:
I liken her to the scorpion,[23]
That flattering, false monstrosity,
Whose face is all sweet courtesy,
While, in the act of flattering,
He with his tail inflicts a sting   640
That spews forth venom; so will she.
She is that spiteful charity
That's false, yet seems as true as steel,

So turneth she hyr false whel
Aboute, for hyt ys nothyng stable –
Now by the fire, now at table;
For many oon hath she thus yblent.
She ys pley of enchauntement,
That semeth oon and ys not soo.
The false thef! What hath she doo,   650
Trowest thou? By oure Lord I wol the seye:

'At the ches with me she gan to pleye;
With hir false draughtes dyvers
She staal on me and tok my fers.
And whan I sawgh my fers awaye,
Allas, I kouthe no lenger playe,
But seyde, "Farewel, swete, ywys,
And farewel al that ever ther ys!"
'Therewith Fortune seyde "Chek her!
And mat in the myd poynt of the checker,   660
With a poun errant!" Allas,
Ful craftier to pley she was
Than Athalus, that made the game
Firsr of the ches, so was hys name.
Bur God wolde I had oones or twyes
Ykoud and knowe the jeupardyes
That kowde the Grek Pictagores!
I shulde have pleyd the bet at ches
And kept my fers the bet therby.
And thogh wherto? For trewely   670
I holde that wyssh nat worth a stree!

And so she turns her lying wheel
Around, for it is never stable;
Now by the fire, now at table,
She's blinded many an eye this way.
Hers is the game enchanters play,
To seem one thing, yet not be one.
The false thief! what then has she done,   650
Think'st thou? Hear, then, what I would say.

The knight describes how Fortune cheated him at chess
and so brought about his ruin.

   'At chess she lured me on to play;
With cheating moves and gambits mean
She stole upon me, took my queen.
And when I saw her swept away,
I lost all sense of how to play
But only said, "Farewell, my bliss,
And farewell all that ever is!"
   'But "checkmate!" was proud Fortune's word,
And "mate" in the centre of the board   660
With a mere travelling pawn! Alas!
Far craftier at the play she was
Than Attalus, who made the game
Of chess; it's said such was his name.
Would God I had, a time or two,
The secrets of the game seen through,
As did the Greek Pythagoras!
I'd have played better chess, alas,
And kept my sweet queen better, too,
And yet, for what? I tell thee true,   670
I hold that wish not worth a flea.

Hyt had be never the bet for me,
For Fortune kan so many a wyle
Ther be but fewe kan hir begile;
And eke she ys the lasse to blame;
Myself I wolde have do the same,
Before God, hadde I ben as she;
She oghte the more excused be.
For this I say yet more therto:
Had I be God and myghte have do   680
My wille whan she my fers kaughte,
I wolde have drawe the same draughte,
For, also wys God yive me reste,
I dar wel swere she took the beste.
But through that draughte I have lorn
My blysse; allas, that I was born!
For evermore, y trowe trewly,
For al my wille, my lust holly
Ys turned; but yet, what to doone?
Be oure Lord, hyt ys to deye soone.   690
For nothyng I leve hyt noght,
But lyve and deye ryght in this thoght;
For there nys planete in firmament,
Ne in ayr ne in erthe noon element,
That they ne yive me a yifte echone
Of wepynge whan I am allone.
For whan that I avise me wel
And bethenke me every del
How that ther lyeth in rekenyng,
In my sorwe, for nothyng,   700
And how ther leveth no gladnesse
May glade me of my distresse,
And how I have lost suffisance,

No better had it been for me
For Fortune has so many a wile,
Few can outwit her, few beguile,
And so she is the less to blame.
Myself, I would have done the same,
By God, had I been such as she:
The more excused she ought to be.
And I can say a lot more, too!
If I'd been God, and so might do   680
My will, when Fortune took my love,
I would have made the selfsame move.
For sure as God shall give me rest,
I dare well say she took the best,
For by that move I'll ever mourn
My bliss – alas that I was born!
For now forever, I think truly,
Despite my will, my joy is wholly
Turned upside down: what's to be done?
It is, by the Lord, to die, and soon.   690
All meaning's gone; I'm left, in short,
To live and die in this same thought.
No planet's in the firmament,
In air or earth no element,
That does not add a gift, each one,
Of weeping, when I am alone,
For when I meditate and scan
And ponder every way I can,
How, in my reckoning of woe,
All has been paid; I nothing owe,   700
And how no gladness yet remains
To bring some joy amid my pains,
And how I've lost all my content,

And therto I have no plesance,
Than may I say I have ryght noght.
And whan al this falleth in my thoght,
Allas, than am I overcome!
For that ys doon ys not to come.
I have more sorowe than Tantale.'
    And whan I herde hym tel thys tale   710
Thus pitously, as I yow telle,
Unnethe myght y lenger dwelle,
Hyt dyde myn herte so moche woo.
'A, goode sir,' quod I, 'say not soo!
Have som pitee on your nature
That formed yow to creature.
Remembre yow of Socrates,
For he ne counted nat thre strees
Of noght that Fortune koude doo.'
    'No,' quod he, 'I kan not soo.'   720
    'Why so, good syr? Yis parde!' quod y;
'Ne say noght so, for trewely,
Thogh ye had lost the ferses twelve,
And ye for sorwe mordred yourselve,
Ye sholde be dampned in this cas
By as good ryght as Medea was,
That slough hir children for Jasoun;
And Phyllis also for Demophoun
Heng hirself – so weylaway! –
For he had broke his terme-day   730
To come to hir. Another rage
Had Dydo, the quene eke of Cartage,
That slough hirself for Eneas
Was fals – which a fool she was!
And Ecquo died for Narcisus

48

And have no mirth, no merriment,
My all is nothing, I may say,
And when I think thus night and day,
Alas, then I am overcome!
For what is done is not to come.
I have more grief than Tantalus.'[24]

    And when I heard him speaking thus   710
So piteously, as I have tried
To tell you, I could scarcely bide
In silence, so much I felt his woe,
But said, 'Ah, good sir, say not so!
Have some pity on your nature –
Nature that formed your every feature –
And call to mind wise Socrates,
He who would never give two peas
For anything Fortune might do.'

    'No,' then said he, 'I'll not do so.'   720

    'Why not, good sir? Say yes,' said I,
'Do not say no, for certainly,
If you had lost some ten or twelve
Queens, and for sorrow killed yourself,
You would be damned, were that the case,
By as good right as Medea was,
That for false Jason her children slew,
And for Demaphoon, Phyllis true
Hanged herself, all her wits astray,
Because he failed the trysting-day   730
He'd vowed to keep. Consider, too,
The queen of Carthage, Dido, who
Counted it death to her to see
Aeneas fleeing – the more fool she![25]
And Echo died because her swain,

Nolde nat love hir, and ryght thus
Hath many another foly doon;
And for Dalida died Sampson,
That slough hymself with a piler.
But ther is no man alyve her   740
Wolde for a fers make this woo!'

'Why so?' quod he, 'hyt ys nat soo.
Thou wost ful lytel what thou menest;
I have lost more than thow wenest.'

'Loo, [sey] how that may be?' quod y;
'Good sir, telle me al hooly
In what wyse, how, why, and wherfore
That ye have thus youre blysse lore.'

'Blythely,' quod he; 'com sytte adoun!
I telle the upon a condicioun   750
That thou shalt hooly, with al thy wyt,
Doo thyn entent to herkene hit.'

'Yis, syr.' 'Swere thy trouthe therto.'

'Gladly.' 'Do thanne holde hereto!'

'I shal ryght blythely, so God me save,
Hooly, with al the wit I have,
Here yow as wel as I kan.'

'A Goddes half!' quod he, and began:

'Syr,' quod he, 'sith first I kouthe
Have any maner wyt fro youthe,   760
Or kyndely understondyng
To comprehende in any thyng
What love was, in myn owne wyt,

50

Narcissus, loved her not again,
And many more have folly done –
Great Samson pulled the pillar down,
And for Delilah perished there –
But there is no man living here   740
Who'd for a chess queen make such woe!'
    'Why not?' said he, 'It is not so.
My loss goes far beyond, my friend,
What thou could'st know or comprehend.'[26]
    'Then say how that may be,' said I,
'Leave nothing out but tell me why,
And in what manner, and by what theft,
You've been so grievously bereft.'
    'Gladly,' said he, 'come, sit by me.
On one condition shall it be,   750
That thou with heart and mind and soul
Hear out my tale, and hear it whole.'
    'Yes, sir!' 'By thine honour, swear it now.'
    'Gladly!' 'Then see thou keep'st thy vow.'
    'So may God save me, willingly
I shall, with my every faculty,
Hear you the very best I can.'
    'So be it!' he said, and then began:

*The knight tells the story of his early youth and how he
first fell in love with his Lady.*

'Sir,' said he, 'when, in earliest youth,
I first could think at all, in truth,   760
Or had the understanding heart
To comprehend in any part
What love was; yet, as I look within,

Dredeles, I have ever yit
Be tributarye and yive rente
To Love, hooly with good entente,
And throgh plesaunce become his thral
With good wille, body, hert, and al.
Al this I putte in his servage,
As to my lord, and dide homage;   770
And ful devoutly I prayed hym to
He shulde besette myn herte so
That hyt plesance to hym were
And worship to my lady dere.

    'And this was longe, and many a yer
Or that myn herte was set owher,
That I dide thus, and nyste why;
I trowe hit cam me kyndely.
Paraunter I was therto most able,
As a whit wal or a table,   780
For hit ys redy to cacche and take
Al that men wil theryn make,
Whethir so men wil portreye or peynte,
Be the werkes never so queynte.

    'And thilke tyme I ferde ryght so,
I was able to have lerned tho,
And to have kend as wel or better,
Paraunter, other art or letre;
But for love cam first in my thoght,
Therfore I forgat hyt noght.   790
I ches love to my firste craft;
Therfore hit ys with me laft,
For-why I tok hyt of so yong age
That malyce hadde my corage
Nat that tyme turned to nothyng

I have no doubt I've ever been
His vassal, who has fully sent
To Love his fief, and paid his rent,
And through delight become his thrall
With good will, body, heart, and all.
All in his service I surrendered
As to my lord, and homage rendered, 770
And with devotion used to pray
He'd set my heart in such a way
As it might please him, as it were,
And honour my sweet lady dear.

  'So for years living in unrest,
Before my heart could end its quest,
I did this, and did not know why;
Perhaps it was natural destiny,
And it was ready, at that age,
Like a blank slate or empty page 780
To take on it, I now believe,
Such marks as anyone might leave,
Whatever they might draw or paint,
No matter how curious or quaint.

  'And all this time I spent in yearning
I could have used for other learning
And might have gained, to fill my mind,
Some art of quite a different kind,
But in my thought love held such power
I could not let it go one hour. 790
Love, then, I chose as my first skill
And therefore it is with me still;
Because so young I took its part
Malice had not yet turned my heart
Into mere nothing, through too great

Thorgh to mochel knowlechyng.
For that tyme Yowthe, my maistresse,
Governed me in ydelnesse;
For hyt was in my firste youthe,
And thoo ful lytel good y couthe,   800
For al my werkes were flyttynge
That tyme, and al my thoght varyinge.
Al were to me ylyche good
That I knew thoo; but thus hit stood:

   'Hit happed that I cam on a day
Into a place ther that I say
Trewly the fayrest companye
Of ladyes that evere man with yë
Had seen togedres in oo place.
Shal I clepe hyt hap other grace   810
That broght me there? Nay, but Fortune,
That ys to lyen ful comune,
The false trayteresse pervers!
God wolde I koude clepe hir wers,
For now she worcheth me ful woo,
And I wol telle sone why soo.

   'Among these ladyes thus echon,
Soth to seyen, y sawgh oon
That was lyk noon of the route;
For I dar swere, withoute doute,   820
That as the someres sonne bryght
Ys fairer, clerer, and hath more lyght
Than any other planete in heven,
The moone or the sterres seven,
For al the world so hadde she
Surmounted hem alle of beaute,
Of maner, and of comlynesse,

Access of knowledge, and its weight.
At that time, Youth, my mistress-wife,
Governed in idleness my life,
For this was in my earliest youth,
When little of good I knew, or truth.   800
Nothing I did could ever last,
My thoughts all muddled, fleeting fast,
And all things seemed of equal good
That I knew then; but thus it stood.

   'One day I chanced to come upon
A place where I had never gone,
And there the loveliest company
Of ladies ever human eye
Had seen together in one place
I saw. And was it luck or grace   810
That led me here? Or Fortune? Aye!
She that in every way will lie,
That traitoress sneering and perverse;
God willing, I could call her worse,
Because she caused me such deep woe,
And I shall tell you now why so.

   'Among these ladies I gazed upon
The truth to tell you, I saw one
That among all the rest stood out;
For I dare say, without a doubt,   820
Just as the summer sun shines bright,
And fairer, clearer, with more light
Than any other star in heaven,
The moon herself, or planets seven,
So she for all the world outshone
Them all, and had them all outdone
In manner and in comeliness,

Of stature, and of wel set gladnesse,
Of goodlyhede so wel beseye –
Shortly, what shal y more seye? 830
By God and by his halwes twelve,
Hyt was my swete, ryght as hirselve.
She had so stedfast countenaunce,
So noble port and meyntenaunce,
And Love, that had wel herd my boone,
Had espyed me thus soone,
That she ful sone in my thoght,
As helpe me God, so was ykaught
So sodenly that I ne tok
No maner counseyl but at hir lok 840
And at myn herte; for-why hir eyen
So gladly, I trow, myn herte seyen
That purely tho myn owne thoght
Seyde hit were beter serve hir for noght
Than with another to be wel.
And hyt was soth, for everydel
I wil anoon ryght telle thee why.

'I sawgh hyr daunce so comlily,
Carole and synge so swetely,
Laughe and pleye so womanly, 850
And loke so debonairly,
So goodly speke and so frendly,
That certes y trowe that evermor
Nas seyn so blysful a tresor.
For every heer on hir hed,
Soth to seyne, hyt was not red,

56

Stature, and modest joyousness,
Gifted with excellence every way –
In short, what more is there to say?   830
By God and all the saints that be,
This was my sweetheart, this was she!
So honest was her face, so bright,
So noble her carriage, so upright,
And Love, that heard my prayer so clearly –
Had seen the way of it so early –
That she at once within my thought
So help me God above, was caught
So suddenly, I never took
Counsel of anything but her look   840
And my own heart, and that because
Joy of her eyes gave me no pause,
And so it was that my own thought
Said: better serve this girl for naught
Than with another pampered live,
And this was true, and I shall give
You *sans* reserve my reasons why.

The knight launches into a paean of praise of the lady.

I saw her dance so prettily,
Carol and sing so charmingly,
Laugh and play so womanly,   850
Look round so debonairly,
Speak friendly and so pleasantly,
That never on this earth, I vow,
Was such a treasure seen till now.
As for the hair upon her head,
To speak precisely, it was not red.

Ne nouther yelowe ne broun hyt nas;
Me thoghte most lyk gold hyt was.
  'And whiche eyen my lady hadde!
Debonaire, goode, glade, and sadde,   860
Symple, of good mochel, noght to wyde.
Therto hir look nas not asyde
Ne overthwert, but beset so wel
Hyt drew and took up everydel
Al that on hir gan beholde.
Hir eyen semed anoon she wolde
Have mercy – fooles wenden soo –
But hyt was never the rather doo.
Hyt nas no countrefeted thyng;
Hyt was hir owne pure lokyng   870
That the goddesse, dame Nature,
Had mad hem opene by mesure
And close; for were she never so glad,
Hyr lokynge was not foly sprad,
Ne wildely, thogh that she pleyde;
But ever, me thoght, hir eyen seyde,
"Be God, my wrathe ys al foryive!"
  'Therwith hir lyste so wel to lyve,
That dulnesse was of hir adrad.
She nas to sobre ne to glad;   880
In aIle thynges more mesure
Had never, I trowe, creature.
But many oon with hire lok she herte,
And that sat hyr ful lyte at herte,
For she knew nothyng of her thoght;
But whether she knew or knew it nowght
Algate she ne roughte of hem a stree! –
To gete her love no ner nas he

Nor brown, nor yellowish like brass:
I thought that most like gold it was.
   'And, oh, what eyes my lady had!
Debonair, kind, if grave or sad,   860
Candid, set evenly, not too wide;
Nor did her glances stray aside
Or sidelong, but were straight and true,
So she could see and well construe
The intent of those who gazed on her.
Sometimes it seemed she might prefer –
Fools reckoned so – among them one,
But, for all that, it was not done.
Here was no counterfeit, no disguise:
These were her own straight-seeing eyes,   870
That goddess Nature caused to be
Opened or closed in modesty;
And though much joy in games she took,
There was no wildness in her look,
Nor foolishness, though she might feign,
But always, I thought, her eyes made plain,
"God knows, my wrath is all in fun!"
   'And, too, she wished to live as one
From whom all dullness flees away.
Never too sober nor too gay;   880
She had a more discerning mind
Than any mortal you might find.
But many with her look she hurt,
And that sat lightly on her heart,
For of her inmost mind she knew
Nothing and whether that be true
Or not, she gave her love no more
To him she knew who lived next door

That woned at hom than he in Ynde;
The formest was alway behynde.   890
But goode folk, over al other,
She loved as man may do hys brother;
Of which love she was wonder large,
In skilful places that bere charge.

    'But which a visage had she thertoo!
Allas, myn herte ys wonder woo
That I ne kan discryven hyt!
Me lakketh both Englyssh and wit
For to undo hyt at the fulle;
And eke my spirites be so dulle   900
So gret a thyng for to devyse.
I have no wit that kan suffise
To comprehende hir beaute.
But thus moche dar I sayn, that she
Was whit, rody, fressh, and lyvely hewed,
And every day hir beaute newed.
And negh hir face was alderbest,
For certes Nature had swich lest
To make that fair that trewly she
Was hir chef patron of beaute,   910
And chef ensample of al hir werk,
And moustre; for be hyt never so derk,
Me thynketh I se hir ever moo.
And yet moreover, thogh alle thoo
That ever livede were now alyve,
Ne sholde have founde to discryve
Yn al hir face a wikked sygne,
For hit was sad, symple, and benygne.

    'And which a goodly, softe speche
Had that swete, my lyves leche!   920

Than to the stranger overseas –
The first was ever the last to please.   890
But good folk, more than any other,
She loved as one might love a brother,
And gave that love in measure large,
Especially at times of weight and charge.
    'With all this such a face had she!
Alas, for my incapacity!
I am so pitifully unfit,
Lacking the English and the wit,
To make you see her face in full;
And, too, my spirits are too dull   900
Such a high purpose to fulfil;
I've neither the talent nor the skill
To limn in truth her beauty free –
But this I do dare say, that she
Was white, fresh, rosy, lively hued,
And all this was each day renewed.
None could come close, and none aspire
To match her, Nature had such desire
To make her fair: she was, I guess,
Chief patron of her loveliness,   910
And chief exemplar of her work,
And pattern, for be it never so dark,
I think I see her ever close,
And yet, moreover, if all those
Who ever lived, were living still,
None ever did, nor ever will
Find in her face a wicked sign,
For all was open, grave, benign.
    'And what a goodly way was hers
Of speaking, my life's leech and nurse,   920

So frendly, and so wel ygrounded,
Up al resoun so wel yfounded,
And so tretable to alle goode
That I dar swere wel, by the roode,
Of eloquence was never founde
So swete a sownynge facounde,
Ne trewer tonged, ne skorned lasse,
Ne bet koude hele – that, by the masse
I durste swere, thogh the pope hit songe,
That ther was never yet throgh hir tonge   930
Man ne woman gretly harmed;
As for her, was al harm hyd –
Ne lasse flaterynge in hir word,
That purely hir symple record
Was founde as trewe as any bond
Or trouthe of any mannes hond;
Ne chyde she koude never a del;
That knoweth al the world ful wel.

'But swich a fairnesse of a nekke
Had that swete that boon nor brekke   940
Nas ther non sene that myssat.
Hyt was whit, smothe, streght, and pure flat,
Wythouten hole or canel-boon,
As be semynge had she noon.
Hyr throte, as I have now memoyre,
Semed a round tour of yvoyre,
Of good gretnesse, and noght to gret.

'And goode faire White she het;
That was my lady name ryght.
She was bothe fair and bryght;   950
She hadde not hir name wrong.
Ryght faire shuldres and body long

Friendly, in learning so well grounded,
And upon reason so well founded,
And so amenable to good
That I dare swear, upon the Rood,
In rhetoric was never heard
Such eloquence in every word,
Nor truer tongued, that used scorn less,
Or better soothed, that, by the mass –
Even one the pope himself had sung –
There was no soul who by her tongue   930
Felt harm or injury unbidden.
And from herself all harm was hidden:
Deceit or flattery she used none –
Her simple promise, and that alone,
As trustworthy and as true was found
As any man's sworn oath and bond.
Nor could she scold, nor could she chide,
And that is known the whole world wide.

'But what a neck had that sweet one!
So beautiful that not a bone   940
Seemed disproportioned; no blemish might
Be seen in it; smooth, straight and white
It was, with such a collarbone
That it appeared that she had none;
Her throat, that in memory I see,
Seemed a round tower of ivory,
Firm, not too large nor yet too slight,

'And people called her "good, fair White",
A name that could not be more right
For her, that fair one shining bright;   950
All others would be false and wrong.
Fair shoulders, waist both slim and long

63

She had, and armes, every lyth
Fattyssh, flesshy, not gret therwith;
Ryght white handes, and nayles rede;
Rounde brestes; and of good brede
Hyr hippes were; a streight flat bak.
I knew on hir noon other lak
That al hir lymmes nere pure sewynge
In as fer as I had knowynge. 960
    'Therto she koude so wel pleye,
Whan that hir lyste, that I dar seye
That she was lyk to torche bryght
That every man may take of lyght
Ynogh, and hyt hath never the lesse.
Of maner and of comlynesse
Ryght so ferde my lady dere,
For every wight of hir manere
Myght cacche ynogh, yif that he wolde,
Yif he had eyen hir to beholde; 970
For I dar swere wel, yif that she
Had among ten thousand be,
She wolde have be, at the leste,
A chef myrour of al the feste,
Thogh they had stonden in a rowe,
To mennes eyen that koude have knowe;
For wher-so men had pleyd or waked,
Me thoghte the felawsshyppe as naked
Withouten hir that sawgh I oones
As a corowne withoute stones. 980
Trewly she was, to myn yë,
The soleyn fenix of Arabye,
For ther livyth never but oon,
Ne swich as she ne knowe I noon.

64

She had; her arms and every limb
Well rounded and well shaped and trim.
Flawless white hands, nails red of hue,
Round breasts, and hips well fashioned, too,
Of proper width; a straight, flat back –
I know of her no flaw or lack
In the proportions of her frame
As far as I could know or name.   960
    'And she could so well laugh and play,
When she so wished, that I dare say
She was a flambeau burning bright,
From which each man could borrow light
Enough, and leave her light no less.
In bearing and in comeliness
So fared my lady, as it were,
That every soul might catch from her
Some of her sprightliness and grace,
If he had eyes to see her face,   970
For I dare say, if she had been
Among ten thousand others seen,
She'd have stood out and shone, at least,
As paragon of all that feast,
Though they had all stood in a row
Before the eyes of men who know
What beauty is; but whether in town or fair
They gathered, their gathering was as bare
Without her that so brightly shone,
As is a crown without a stone.   980
Truly she was, to my own eye,
The unique phoenix of Araby,
For of that kind there lives but one,
Nor such as she was, I know none.

'To speke of godnesse, trewly she
Had as moche debonairte
As ever had Hester in the Bible,
And more, yif more were possyble.
And soth to seyne, therwythal
She had a wyt so general,   990
So hool enclyned to alle goode,
That al hir wyt was set, by the rode,
Withoute malyce, upon gladnesse;
And therto I saugh never yet a lesse
Harmful than she was in doynge.
I sey nat that she ne had knowynge
What harm was, or elles she
Had koud no good, so thinketh me.

'And trewly for to speke of trouthe,
But she had had, hyt hadde be routhe.   1000
Therof she had so moche hyr del –
And I dar seyn and swere hyt wel –
That Trouthe hymself over al and al
Had chose hys maner principal
In hir that was his restyng place.
Therto she hadde the moste grace
To have stedefast perseveraunce
And esy, atempre governaunce
That ever I knew or wyste yit,
So pure suffraunt was hir wyt;   1010
And reson gladly she understood;
Hyt folowed wel she koude good.
She used gladly to do wel;
These were hir maners everydel.

'Therwith she loved so wel ryght
She wrong do wolde to no wyght.

'To speak of goodness, truly she
Had as much grace and charity
As Esther[27] had, whose tale we read
In Scripture – perhaps more, indeed,
And, truth to tell, she had a mind
Of such a generous, open kind,   990
So given to all that's good and fair
That it was wholly set, I swear,
On happiness from malice free,
And never, truly, did I see
A soul more harmless in her doing.
I do not say she had no knowing
Of what harm was, or else she could
Not know so well the true and good.

'And now indeed to speak of truth,
If she'd not had it from her youth,   1000
It had been grievous; but thereof
She had, in fact, so great a trove
That Truth himself his dwelling chose,
His own chief manor, park, and close,
In her that was his resting place.
Too, she had more of that good grace
To persevere and steadfast stand,
Yet govern with an easy hand,
That ever I saw in human kind.
So large and generous was her mind,   1010
Reason she gladly understood;
It followed that she loved the good,
So to do well was joy to her,
And such this lady's manners were.

'Now add her passion deep and strong
For right, for no one could she wrong,

No wyght myghte do hir noo shame,
She loved so wel hir owne name.
Hyr lust to holde no wyght in honde,
Ne, be thou siker, she wolde not fonde   1020
To holde no wyght in balaunce
By half word ne by countenaunce –
But if men wolde upon hir lye –
Ne sende men into Walakye,
To Pruyse, and into Tartarye,
To Alysaundre, ne into Turkye,
And byd hym faste anoon that he
Goo hoodles into the Drye Se
And come horn by the Carrenar,
And seye, "Sir, be now ryght war   1030
That I may of yow here seyn
Worshyp or that ye come ageyn!"
She ne used no suche knakkes smale.
    'But wherfore that y telle my tale?
Ryght on thys same, as I have seyd,
Was hooly al my love leyd;
For certes she was, that swete wif,
My suffisaunce, my lust, my lyf,
Myn hap, myn hele, and al my blesse,
My worldes welfare, and my goddesse,   1040
And I hooly hires and everydel.'

    'By oure Lord,' quod I, 'y trowe yow wel!
Hardely, your love was wel beset;
I not how ye myghte have do bet.'

Nor yet from any suffer shame,
So well she loved her own good name.
Nor wished she falsely to cajole,
Nor, be assured, wished any soul   1020
To suffer long-drawn-out suspense
Through sly half-truths or inference
(But she'd not suffer slanders vile),
Nor to Wallachia men exile[28]
To Russia or far Mongolia,
Egypt or Anatolia,[29]
And bid him forthwith cross the dread
Dry Sea,[30] with bare, uncovered head,
And come home by the Kara-Nor,[31]
And say, "Now, sir, you may be sure,   1030
With honour must your name resound
Before I hear you're homeward bound."
To such mean tricks she'd not descend.
    'But why do I tell thee this, my friend?
On this same lady, thou must know,
My love I wholly did bestow,
For she was surely – that sweet wife –
My sustenance, my love, my life,
All my well-being, all that's best,
My world's welfare, my goddess blessed,   1040
I wholly hers to my life's end.'

The dreamer provokes the knight to ever more fervent
protestations.

    'Now, by our Lord, I comprehend,'
I said, 'your love was well begun;
You scarcely could have better done.'

69

'Bet? Ne no wyght so wel,' quod he.
'Y trowe hyt wel, sir,' quod I, 'parde!'
'Nay, leve hyt wel!' 'Sire, so do I;
I leve row wel, that trewely
Yow thoghte that she was the beste
And to beholde the alderfayreste,   1050
Whoso had loked hir with your eyen.'
    'With myn? Nay, alle that hir seyen
Seyde and sworen hyt was soo.
And thogh they ne hadde, I wolde thoo
Have loved best my lady free,
Thogh I had had al the beaute
That ever had Alcipyades,
And al the strengthe of Ercules,
And therto had the worthynesse
Of Alysaunder, and al the rychesse   1060
That ever was in Babyloyne,
In Cartage, or in Macedoyne,
Or in Rome, or in Nynyve;
And therto also hardy be
As was Ector, so have I joye,
That Achilles slough at Troye –
And therfore was he slayn alsoo
In a temple, for bothe twoo
Were slayne, he and Antylegyus
(And so seyth Dares Frygius),   1070
For love of Polixena –
Or ben as wis as Mynerva,
I wolde ever, withoute drede,
Have loved hir, for I moste nede.
"Nede?" Nay, trewly, I gabbe now;
Noght "nede," and I wol tellen how:

'Better? no man so well,' said he.
'I know it,' said I, 'perfectly.'
'No, grant it now!' 'Sir, so I do;
I grant indeed that truly you
Believed she was the best and dearest,
And to behold the very fairest   1050
To all who saw her with your eyes.'

    'With mine? No, all, I tell no lies,
Who saw her swore in that same vein;
But if they had not, even then
I would have loved my lady blessed
Though all the beauty I possessed
Of the young Alcibiades[32]
And all the strength of Hercules,
And more than that the high estate
Of Alexander, and all the riches great   1060
Stored up in Babylonia,
In Carthage or Macedonia,
In Rome or ancient Ninevah,
And had been, too, as strong in war
As Hector was, so I have joy,
Who slew Achilles in bloody Troy,
And so he too was slain, within
A temple, with his friend and kin,
A soldier named Archilogus,
(For so says Dares Frygius[33])   1070
For love of Polixena's eyes;[34]
Or had been as Minerva, wise,
I would, I swear to you indeed,
Have loved that maid for my great need.
"Need"! oh, I babble like a lout –
Not "need"! – here's how it came about:

71

For of good wille myn herte hyt wolde,
And eke to love hir I was holde
As for the fairest and the beste.
She was as good, so have I reste,   1080
As ever was Penelopee of Grece,
Or as the noble wif Lucrece,
That was the beste – he telleth thus,
The Romayn, Tytus Lyvyus –
She was as good, and nothyng lyk
(Thogh hir stories be autentyk),
Algate she was as trewe as she.
    'But wherfore that I telle thee
Whan I first my lady say?
I was ryght yong, soth to say,   1090
And ful gret nede I hadde to lerne;
Whan my herte wolde yerne
To love, hyt was a gret empryse.
But as my wyt koude best suffise,
After my yonge childly wyt,
Withoute drede, I besette hyt
To love hir in my beste wyse,
To do hir worship and the servise
That I koude thoo, be my trouthe,
Withoute feynynge outher slouthe,   1100
For wonder feyn I wolde hir se.
So mochel hyt amended me
That whan I saugh hir first a-morwe
I was warished of al my sorwe
Of al day after; til hyt were eve
Me thoghte nothyng myghte me greve,
Were my sorwes never so smerte.
And yet she syt so in myn herte

By will my heart would hold her fast,
Told me to love her to the last,
Who was the fairest and the best.
She was as good, so I have rest,   1080
As was Penelope[35] of Greece,
Or as the noble wife Lucrece,[36]
That was the best: he tells it thus –
The Roman, Titus Livius,
But she as good, though not the same,
Although the stories of her fame
Were all authentic, yet the one
I speak of was no less.   But on
With my sad tale. When I first saw
My lady, I was young and raw,   1090
And a great need I had to learn;
And when my heart began to yearn
To love, it was a great emprise.
But as my mind could best devise,
And with such wit as I then knew,
I managed, past all question, to
Love her the best that I could do,
Pay honour and all service due
That then I could; yes, by my troth,
Without pretence and without sloth,   1100
For I so longed my love to see,
And so much joy it brought to me,
To see her face when it was dawn,
That all my woes were cured and gone
For that whole day, till light should wane,
Nothing, I thought, could cause me pain,
However great my sorrow's smart.
And she still lived so in my heart,

That, by my trouthe, y nolde noght
For al thys world out of my thoght 1110
Leve my lady; noo, trewely!'

    'Now, by my trouthe, sir,' quod I,
'Me thynketh ye have such a chaunce
As shryfte wythoute repentaunce.'

    'Repentaunce? Nay, fy!' quod he,
'Shulde y now repente me
To love? Nay, certes, than were I wel
Wers than was Achitofel,
Or Anthenor, so have I joye,
The traytor that betraysed Troye, 1120
Or the false Genelloun,
He that purchased the tresoun
Of Rowland and of Olyver.
Nay, while I am alyve her,
I nyl foryete hir never moo.'

    'Now, goode syre,' quod I thoo,
'Ye han wel told me herebefore;
Hyt ys no nede to reherse it more,
How ye sawe hir first, and where.
But wolde ye tel me the manere 1130
To hire which was your firste speche –
Therof I wolde yow beseche –
And how she knewe first your thoght,
Whether ye loved hir or noght?
And telleth me eke what ye have lore,
I herde yow telle herebefore.'

    'Yee!' seyde he, 'thow nost what thow menest;
I have lost more than thou wenest.'
'What los ys that?' quod I thoo;
'Nyl she not love yow? Ys hyt soo? 1140

That, in all truth, I could not well
Out of my mind her thought dispel 1110
And so go from her – no, not her!'
    'Now I believe,' I said, 'good sir,
That chance has so much favoured you
As shrive you *sans* repentance due.'[37]
    'Repentance?' he said, 'fie on that!'
And shall I now repent – for what?
For loving her? then I were well
Worse than the base Achitophel[38]
Or Antenor, so I have joy,
The traitor who betrayed proud Troy, 1120
Or the foul, faithless Ganelon,
Who for base bribery brought down
Roland and Oliver to their death.[39]
No! while I love and still draw breath,
I'll not forget her till I die!'
    'Oh, well now, my good sir,' said I,
'You have described to me before –
There's no need to rehearse it more –
How you first saw the girl, and tarried,
But, rather, tell me how you carried 1130
Yourself toward her in your first speech –
That's what I chiefly would beseech
Of you – how first she knew your thought,
And whether you loved or loved her not?
And tell me of your loss once more,
Of which I've heard you tell before.'
    'Too true; thou know'st not what thou meanest,'
Said he, 'It is far more than thou weenest.'
'What loss is that?' I answered then,
'Won't she return your love again? 1140

Or have ye oght doon amys,
That she hath left yow? Ys hyt this?
For Goddes love, telle me al.'
    'Before God,' quod he, 'and I shal.
I saye ryght as I have seyd,
On hir was al my love leyd,
And yet she nyste hyt nat, never a del
Noght longe tyme, leve hyt wel!
For be ryght siker, I durste noght
For al this world telle hir my thoght,   1150
Ne I wolde have wraththed hir, trewely.
For wostow why? She was lady
Of the body; she had the herte,
And who hath that may not asterte.
But for to kepe me fro ydelnesse,
Trewly I dide my besynesse
To make songes, as I best koude,
And ofte tyme I song hem loude;
And made songes thus a gret del,
Althogh I koude not make so wel   1160
Songes, ne knewe the art al,
As koude Lamekes sone Tubal,
That found out first the art of songe;
For as hys brothres hamers ronge
Upon hys anvelt up and doun,
Therof he took the firste soun –
But Grekes seyn Pictagoras,
That he the firste fynder was
Of the art (Aurora telleth so);
But therof no fors of hem two.   1170
Algates songes thus I made
Of my felynge, myn herte to glade;

Or did you say some words amiss
That made her leave you? Is it this?
Dear sir, for God's sake tell me all.'

   'Before God,' said he, 'that I shall.
Again I say as I have said,
Wholly on her my love was laid,
Yet she knew nothing, did not see
A long time, how it was with me.
Believe me, sir, for I would not
For all this world, tell her my thought   1150
Nor give her cause, upon my honour,
For anger – why? she was my owner.
Body and heart lay in her keeping,
And who has that has no escaping.
But, to keep idleness at bay,
I occupied myself each day
With making songs as best I could
To sing aloud, and so I would.
So many songs I made, but still
Never attained the highest skill   1160
In song-making, nor mastery won
Of that whole art, like Lamech's son,
Tubal,[40] who first invented song,
For, as his brother's hammer rung
Upon his anvil, pound on pound,
He took from it the primal sound –
Greeks say Pythagoras was the one
By whom this art was first begun –
At least, Aurora[41] says it's true –
But never mind about those two.   1170
I made my ditties to give voice
To what I felt, and to rejoice;

And, lo, this was [the] altherferste –
I not wher hyt were the werste.

'Lord, hyt maketh myn herte lyght
Whan I thenke on that swete wyght
That is so semely on to see;
And wisshe to God hit myghte so bee
That she wolde holde me for hir knyght,
My lady, that is so fair and bryght!'   1180

'Now have I told thee, soth to say,
My firste song. Upon a day
I bethoghte me what woo
And sorwe that I suffred thoo
For hir, and yet she wyste hyt noght,
Ne telle hit durste I nat my thoght.
"Allas," thoghte I, "y kan no red;
And but I telle hir, I nam but ded;
And yif I telle hyr, to seye ryght soth,
I am adred she wol be wroth.   1190
Allas, what shal I thanne do?"
    'In this debat I was so wo
Me thoghte myn herte braste atweyne!
So at the laste, soth to sayne,
I bethoghte me that Nature
Ne formed never in creature
So moche beaute, trewely,
And bounte, wythoute mercy.
In hope of that, my tale I tolde

78

So listen, sir, here's the very first –
I don't know if it be the worst:

'O Lord, it makes my heart so light,
To think upon that sweetest wight
That is so beautiful to see;
And I wish to God that it might be
That she would have me for her knight,
My lady, that is so fair and bright.　　　　　　　1180

The knight tells how he came to confess his love to the lady;
the dreamer asks one last question.

'Now I have told thee, truth to say,
My earliest song. And then, one day,
I took to thinking on what pain
And sorrow I'd endured in vain
For her, and yet she knew it not,
Nor did I dare to speak my thought.
"Oh, which way shall I turn?" I said:
"Unless I tell her, I am dead,
But if I speak straight out, I'm sure
It will most likely anger her,　　　　　　　1190
God knows, and then what shall I do?"
  'In this debate I had such woe
I thought my heart would break in two,
So at the last, I tell thee true,
Into my mind there came the thought
That surely Nature never wrought
In one of hers such loveliness
And grace, yet left it merciless.
And in that hope I then let fall

79

With sorwe, as that I never sholde,   1200
For nedes, and mawgree my hed,
I most have told hir or be ded.
I not wel how that I began;
Ful evel rehersen hyt I kan;
And eke, as helpe me God withal,
I trowe hyt was in the dismal,
That was the ten woundes of Egipte –
For many a word I over-skipte
In my tale, for pure fere
Lest my wordes mysset were.   1210
With sorweful herte and woundes dede,
Softe and quakynge for pure drede
And shame, and styntynge in my tale
For ferde, and myn hewe al pale –
Ful ofte I wex bathe pale and red –
Bowynge to hir, I heng the hed;
I durste nat ones loke hir on,
For wit, maner, and al was goon.
I seyde "Mercy!" and no more.
Hyt nas no game; hyt sat me sore.   1220
    'So at the laste, soth to seyn,
Whan that myn hert was come ageyn,
To telle shortly al my speche,
With hool herte I gan hir beseche
That she wolde be my lady swete;
And swor, and gan hir hertely hete
Ever to be stedfast and trewe,
And love hir alwey fresshly newe,
And never other lady have,
And al hir worship for to save   1230
As I best koude. I swor hir this:

My tale, but clumsily, and all   1200
Against my will, and for sheer need –
I had to speak, or die indeed.
How I began to speak, and how
Continued, I can't remember now,
And even, so help me God, I thought
I must be in the "dismal"[42] caught,
With Egypt's ten plagues, without doubt,
For many a word did I leave out
In my telling, in panic frozen
Lest my words might be ill chosen.   1210
All heartsore, wounded like one dead,
Timid, and shaking for pure dread
And shame, and halting in my tale,
For fear, and with complexion pale –
Often, in fact, both pale and red –
Bowing to her, I hung my head.
Her face I dared not look upon,
For breeding, intellect, all were gone.
I said "Mercy!" and no more;
This was no game, but anguish sore.   1220
    'So at the last, to tell you plain,
When my heart was up again,
All that I finally said, good sir –
With all my heart I begged of her
To be my own dear lady sweet,
And swore, as long as my heart beat,
Ever to be steadfast and true,
And love her always fresh and new,
And never another lady have,
And her high honour always save,   1230
As best I could. And I swore this:

81

"For youres is alle that ever ther ys
For evermore, myn herte swete!
And never to false yow, but I mete,
I nyl, as wys God helpe me soo!"

'And whan I had my tale y-doo,
God wot, she acounted nat a stree
Of al my tale, so thoghte me.
To telle shortly ryght as hyt ys,
Trewly hir answere hyt was this –   1240
I kan not now wel counterfete
Hir wordes, but this was the grete
Of hir answere: she sayde "Nay"
Al outerly. Allas, that day
The sorowe I suffred and the woo
That trewly Cassandra, that soo
Bewayled the destruccioun
Of Troye and of Ilyoun,
Had never swich sorwe as I thoo.
I durste no more say thertoo   1250
For pure fere, but stal away;
And thus I lyved ful many a day,
That trewely I hadde no ned
Ferther than my beddes hed
Never a day to seche sorwe;
I fond hyt redy every morwe,
For-why I loved hyr in no gere.

'So hit befel, another yere
I thoughte ones I wolde fonde
To do hir knowe and understonde   1260
My woo; and she wel understod
That I ne wilned thyng but god,
And worship, and to kepe hir name

82

"For yours is all that ever is
For ever more, my own heart sweet,
And never, save by a dream's deceit
Shall I be false, God helping me!"

'And when I had so spoken, she
Accounted not a straw, God knows,
Of all my tale, so I suppose.
And now, to speak briefly as it is,
I'll give her answer: it was this –   1240
I can't repeat it word for word,
But here's the gist of what I heard
Of her reply: She just said "No!"
And utterly. Dear God, the woe
And grief I suffered then! I know
Even Cassandra, who did so
Bewail the bitter tearing down
Of Troy and ancient Ilion,
Had no such sorrow as I had then.
I did not dare to speak again   1250
Out of pure fear, but stole away,
And thus I lived for many a day;
And truly, I had little need
To leave my own bedside indeed
Each day to seek out grief and mourning;
I found them waiting every morning,
So changelessly I loved my dear.

'So it fell out, another year,
I thought once more I'd try to show
My pain to her, so she would know   1260
It all, and so she truly could
See that I only willed her good,
And honoured and held high her name,

Over alle thynges, and drede hir shame,
And was so besy hyr to serve,
And pitee were I shulde sterve,
Syth that I wilned noon harm, ywis.
So whan my lady knew al this,
My lady yaf me al hooly
The noble yifte of hir mercy, 1270
Savynge hir worship by al weyes –
Dredles, I mene noon other weyes.
And therwith she yaf me a ryng;
I trowe hyt was the firste thyng;
But if myn herte was ywaxe
Glad, that is no nede to axe!
As helpe me God, I was as blyve
Reysed as fro deth to lyve –
Of al happes the alderbeste,
The gladdest, and the moste at reste. 1280
For trewely that swete wyght,
Whan I had wrong and she the ryght,
She wolde alway so goodly
Foryeve me so debonairly.
In al my yowthe, in al chaunce,
She took me in hir governaunce,
Therwyth she was alway so trewe
Our joye was ever ylyche newe;
Oure hertes wern so evene a payre
That never nas that oon contrayre 1290
To that other for no woo.
For sothe, ylyche they suffred thoo
Oo blysse and eke oo sorwe bothe;
Ylyche they were bothe glad and wrothe;
Al was us oon, withoute were.

And hated what might cause it shame,
And, serving her, stood ever by:
A pity then, that I should die,
Seeing that harm I could not do.
So, when she saw all this was true,
My lady dear then gave to me
A noble gift, her mercy free,   1270
Save for her honour, pure and true –
No other means or way would do.
With this as well she gave a ring –
Of all she gave me, the first thing;
But if my heart with joy did swell,
No need to ask, no need to tell!
It was as though I had been raised
From death to life, may God be praised!
Of all life's happenings the best,
The gladdest and most full of rest;   1280
For always would my dear delight,
When I was wrong and she was right,
Always so goodly and so free,
Forgive me debonairly. She,
In all my youth, in every chance,
Took me under her governance;
And altogether was so true,
Our joy seemed ever fresh and new;
Our hearts were paired together so
They never contrary would go   1290
One to the other; and if ill
Should chance, they suffered with one will.
One gladness and one sorrow they
Together felt, if sad or gay.
With us all things were one, no fear,

And thus we lyved ful many a yere
So wel I kan nat telle how.'
   'Sir,' quod I, 'where is she now?'
   'Now?' quod he, and stynte anoon.
Therwith he wax as ded as stoon   1300
And seyde, 'Allas, that I was bore!
That was the los that here-before
I tolde the that I hadde lorn.
Bethenke how I seyde here-beforn,
"Thow wost ful lytel what thow menest;
I have lost more than thow wenest."
God wot, allas! Ryght that was she!'
   'Allas, sir, how? What may that be?'
   'She ys ded' 'Nay!' 'Yis, be my trouthe!'
   'Is that youre los? Be God, hyt ys routhe!'   1310
And with that word ryght anoon
They gan to strake forth; al was doon,
For that tyme, the hert-huntyng.
   With that me thoghte that this kyng
Gan homwarde for to ryde
Unto a place, was there besyde,
Which was from us but a lyte –
A long castel with walles white,
Be Seynt Johan, on a ryche hil,
As me mette; but thus hyt fil.   1320
Ryght thus me mette, as I yow telle,
That in the castell ther was a belle,
As hyt hadde smyten houres twelve.
Therwyth I awook myselve
And fond me lyinge in my bed;
And the book that I hadde red,
Of Alcione and Seys the kyng,

And thus we lived for many a year
So well, I cannot tell you how.'
   'Sir,' I said then, 'Where is she now?'
   'Now?' said the knight, and thereupon
He stopped as dead as any stone.   1300
'Alas, that I was born!' said he,
'That was the loss I told to thee,
That I with such deep sorrow bore.
Take thought to what I said before:
"*Thou know'st full little what thou meanest;*
I have lost more than thou weenest."
God knows, alas! that loss was she!'
   'Alas, sir, how? How may that be?'
   'She is dead!' 'No!' 'Yes, by my truth!'
   'Is that your loss? By God, it is ruth!'   1310
And with that word the horn anon
Sounded for home, and all was done
Of hunting of the hart that day.
   With that, it seemed, the king straightway[43]
Began to ride toward home, which was
A place not very far from us,
But a small distance from our sight;
It was a long castle with walls of white[44]
On a rich hill – Saint John's, it seemed,[45]
And so it happened while I dreamed.   1320
And so I dreamed what now I tell:
That in that castle there was a bell:
Twelve hours it struck; and when that stroke
I heard, I suddenly awoke,
And found myself upon my bed
And the book that I had read
Of Alcyone and Ceyx her spouse,

And of the goddes of slepyng,
I fond hyt in myn hond ful even.
Thoghte I, 'Thys ys so queynt a sweven   1330
That I wol, be processe of tyme,
Fonde to put this sweven in ryme
As I kan best, and that anoon.'
This was my sweven; now hit ys doon.

Explicit the Bok of the Duchesse

And of the lord of slumber's house,
I found still open in my fingers.
I thought, 'This dream so strangely lingers   1330
That I will, in the course of time,
Try to set it down in rhyme
As best I can, and do it soon.'
This was my dream; now it is done.

1. The eight-year sickness and the 'one physician' have been the subjects of much debate, but the likelihood is that it refers to the 'sickness' caused by unrequited love. For an interesting discussion of this, see *Riverside,* Explanatory Note to lines 30–43, p. 967.

2. The book appears to have been Ovid's *Metamorphoses*, Book XI of which tells the story of Ceyx and Alcyone. Chaucer greatly condensed and modified Ovid's original, and completely omitted the ending, in which the two are changed into a pair of seabirds for whom the sea is made calm and peaceful during the week in which the female bird is brooding over her young. Alcyone's name lives on in our word 'halcyon'.

3. 'game of tables', i.e., backgammon.

4. 'law of kind', i.e., the Natural Law, which was understood to have prevailed on earth until the coming of Christ; it may refer to a Golden Age in which such modern vices as greed, hatred, the desire for conquest, etc., were thought to be unknown. Chaucer's short poem 'The Former Age' is one of the most perfect expressions of this idea.

5. i.e., the Mediterranean.

6. Ambrosius Theodosius Macrobius, late fourth- to early fifth-century Latin writer and philosopher. His commentary on Cicero's *Dream of Scipio* was well known to Chaucer and his contemporaries; see especially Chaucer's *Parliament of Fowls*.

7. Publus Cornelius Scipio Africanus, 236–183 BC, a great Roman general and conqueror of Hannibal in the Punic Wars. He was given the honorary title of 'Africanus' following his victories in Africa.

8. Lamedon, father of Priam.

9. Medea and Aeson's son was Jason, winner of the Golden Fleece.

10. Lavinia, Italian princess whom Aeneas wed after deserting Dido; see *The Legend of Good Women* for Chaucer's version of this story.

11. Gloss, a running commentary on the poem.

12. Octavian, Augustus Caesar: Skeat, in his edition of Chaucer (1894), thought this might be an oblique compliment to King Edward III, during whose reign the poem was composed. Others hold that the reference is to Gaunt, with various implications as to the dating of the poem since it was only after his second marriage (to Constance of Castile) in September 1371 that Gaunt took on the title of King of Castile and Leon.

13. Zephyr, the West Wind.

14. Algus, Old French adaptation of the name Al Khwarizmi, who was a ninth-century mathematician and originator of the decimal system later to be adopted throughout Europe.

15. The 'complaint', a kind of love-lament, is found frequently in the works of medieval poets. V.J. Scattergood points out that the lament 'is not a form…but a type of expression. It is a lament for some loss incurred or injustice suffered or grief experienced' (A.J. Minnis, ed., Oxford Guides to Chaucer, *The Shorter Poems*, Oxford, 1995, p. 465).

16. 'Without notes and without song': this line indicates that Chaucer may have been familiar with an aspect of French medieval poetics that distinguished between 'artificial music'– music accompanying a song or lyric and intended for performance – and 'natural music'– the poetic words alone, without accompaniment, and intended for private or solitary recital. The songs of lament sung by the man in black as he mused alone in the depths of the forest might well serve as an example of such 'natural music'.

17. 'god of kind': i.e., god of all living creatures.

18. The reference is to Ovid's *Remedia Amoris* ('Remedies of Love').

19. According to legend, Orpheus, the supreme musician, was the son of Calliope, the Muse of music.

20. Daedalus: in Greek mythology, master of mechanical inventions, builder of the labyrinth of Minos, King of Crete, and maker of a pair of wings that enabled him to escape from the imprisonment to which Minos had condemned him.

21. Galen and Hippocrates, ancient Greek physicians much venerated in the Middle Ages and beyond.

22. Sisyphus, in Greek mythology, was condemned to an eternity of rolling a heavy boulder up a steep hill only to have it fall back again as soon as it reached the top.

23. Medieval authors frequently used the scorpion as a symbol of treachery.

24. According to legend, Tantalus was condemned to suffer in Hades by being placed in a pool of water overhung by fruit trees, both of which, the water and the fruit, would instantly shrink back just out of reach whenever he tried to drink the water or pluck the fruit..

25. The stories of Medea, Phyllis, and Dido are all told, among others, in Chaucer's *The Legend of Good Women*.

26. These lines are repeated three times in the poem. Here they are somewhat modernised; in lines 1137–38 and 1305–06 they are given in Chaucer's original language, with slightly modified spelling.

27. For Esther, see the Old Testament book of Esther. Traditionally, Queen Esther was held up as a supreme model of feminine virtue.

28. This and the following eight lines are especially interesting for what Chaucer is saying about certain aspects of *fin' amors*, a fundamental requirement of which was the rendering of unconditional service by the lover to the lady. Here, the knight describes the sort of next-to-impossible ordeal that might be demanded by a capricious and cruel mistress, behaviour in utter opposition to the whole mental and spiritual outlook of Blanche the duchess.

29. Anatolia: substituted for Chaucer's 'Turkye' for the sake of the rhyme.

30. 'Dry Sea': probably the Gobi desert.

31. Chaucer's word is 'Carrenar', a desolate place located on the east side of the Gobi.

32. Alcibiades (d. *c*.404 BC), Athenian general and politician.

33. Dares the Phrygian or Dares the Trojan. A work on the Trojan War was ascribed to him.

34. Polixena, sister of Troilus: see *Troilus and Cressida,* Chaucer's great narrative poem of a passionate and doomed love affair set in the context of the Trojan War.

35. Penelope, Queen of Ithaca and wife of Odysseus, who, during his long absence from home, remained faithful despite constant harassment by a crowd of scheming, so-called 'suitors', bent on persuading her that her husband would never return and that she should therefore renounce her marriage in order that one of them could become her new 'husband'.

36. Lucrece's story is told in Chaucer's *The Legend of Good Women*; see also Shakespeare's poem *The Rape of Lucrece.*

37. To 'shrive' was to give someone absolution after confession of sin. The dreamer seems to be implying, perhaps ironically, that the knight has got away with, or has been awarded, more good fortune than he deserves. The line has been the subject of various scholarly interpretations; however, it's possible to catch a whiff of the confessional in all of the knight's soul-baring to the dreamer.

38. Achitophel: in the Old Testament, wicked counsellor to King David. Absolom, the king's son, allied himself with Achitophel in rebellion against the king.

39. Roland, hero of the eleventh-century *Chanson de Roland*, best known of the French *chansons de geste*, and Oliver, his comrade and brother-in-arms, were both betrayed by the evil turncoat Ganelon.

40. The ascription should have been to Jubal (Genesis 4:21), not Tubal; this was a frequent misreading by medieval writers.

41. Aurora: title of a twelfth-century commentary on the Bible by Peter of Riga.

42. An interesting discussion of the 'dismal' and its connection with the ten '*woundes*', or plagues, of Egypt is given in *Riverside*, Explanatory Note 1206–07, p. 975. The word 'dismal' may be derived from Old French *dis mal*, (unlucky days), though its origin is more likely to be Latin, *decem mali* (ten evils). In the Middle Ages, two days of each month were called 'Egyptian days' and considered unlucky; they were sometimes called 'dismal days'. In the lines above, Chaucer is playing with this idea for his own purposes.

43. Riverside, Explanatory Note p. 976, suggests that the Emperor Octavian (line 368), the man in black, and this king are all representations of Gaunt. See also note 12 above.

44. 'long castle': a play on John of Gaunt's title, 'Duke of Lancaster'; 'walls of white': a reference to the name of the duchess, Blanche, or 'White'.

45. 'rich hill,' i.e., Richmond. John of Gaunt became Earl of Richmond in infancy, and the estate belonged to him until 1372. 'Saint John': John of Gaunt's name saint.

BIOGRAPHICAL NOTE

Geoffrey Chaucer was born between 1340 and 1344, the son of John Chaucer, a London vintner, and his wife Agnes. Little is known of his life before 1357, when he was serving as a page in the household of Prince Lionel. In 1359 he went to France with Edward III's army to fight in the Hundred Years War. He was taken prisoner, but released after the Treaty of Brétigny in 1360. Around this time it is believed that he produced his first literary work, a translation of the French allegory *Roman de la Rose*. During the 1360s he married Philippa Roet, lady-in-waiting to Queen Philippa and sister to John of Gaunt's future wife. Philippa died in 1387, but Chaucer continued to enjoy Gaunt's patronage, and in 1369 he wrote *The Book of the Duchess*, lamenting the death of Gaunt's wife.

He entered the king's service and held a number of positions at Court. Between 1367 and 1378, he was sent on several diplomatic missions, and during this time he travelled to Italy, where he became acquainted with the works of Giovanni Boccaccio and Francis Petrarch. It is believed it was the influence of Dante that inspired him to write in the vernacular rather than the French of the Court. Around 1385 he moved to Kent, where he was appointed justice of the peace, and this coincided with a period of considerable creativity, with Chaucer producing some of the best of his poetic works, including *Troilus and Criseyde* (*c.*1385). He began his most famous work, *The Canterbury Tales*, in approximately 1387. This vast work, chronicling the lives and stories of a group of pilgrims travelling to the shrine of Thomas à Becket, was never in fact completed, but it remains perhaps the most important literary work of the age.

Chaucer died in 1400 and was buried in Westminster Abbey.

E.B. ('Lyn') Richmond is a member of the New Chaucer Society, and has had a lifelong fascination with Chaucer. Her interests include Shakespeare, translating French poetry and writing her own verse. She has previously translated Chaucer's *The Parliament of Birds*, also published by Hesperus Press.